D0349155

,1-M

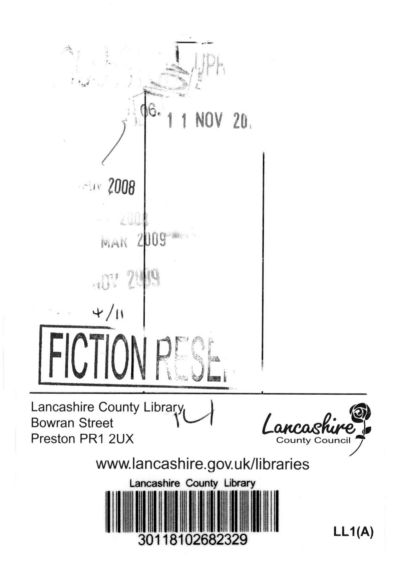

06. 1 1 NOV 20.

2008

2008

MAR 2009

NOV 2009

4/11

FICTION RESE

Lancashire County Library
Bowran Street
Preston PR1 2UX

Lancashire
County Council

www.lancashire.gov.uk/libraries

Lancashire County Library

30118102682329

LL1(A)

Heart of Fire

Heart of Fire

Maxine Barry

ROBERT HALE · LONDON

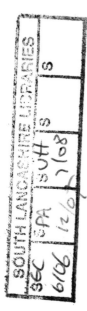

© Maxine Barry 2006
First published in Great Britain 2006

ISBN-10: 0-7090-7992-3
ISBN-13: 978-0-7090-7992-7

Robert Hale Limited
Clerkenwell House
Clerkenwell Green
London EC1R 0HT

The right of Maxine Barry to be identified as
author of this work has been asserted by her
in accordance with the Copyright, Designs and
Patents Act 1988.

2 4 6 8 10 9 7 5 3 1

LANCASHIRE COUNTY LIBRARY	
10268232	
HJ	15/06/2006
F	£18.99

Typeset in 11/16pt New Century Schoolbook
by Derek Doyle & Associates, Shaw Heath
Printed in Great Britain by St Edmundsbury Press
Bury St Edmunds, Suffolk
Bound by Woolnough Bookbinding Limited

Many thanks to Dick Greening, for his help in researching this novel

Foreword by the Author

I should like to point out that all characters depicted within this novel are fictional, as are any 'historical' references to the heroine's Hawaiian royal family. Even the volcano, Kulahaleha, is a figment of my imagination, and should not be compared to any other Hawaiian volcano! Only the mythological references correspond to proper Hawaiian deities.

Prologue

Hawaii – a long, long time ago

The man, naked and proud, gazed upwards in awe-struck wonder as the sky around him seemed to erupt in a massive burst of orange flame. He felt the heat, as a wall of burning air, hit him, almost knocking him off his feet and turning his already bronzed skin to a painful red. And still he climbed on, higher and higher up the precipitous slope, wanting only to get closer to her.

She who had haunted his dreams for as long as he could remember.

Far below him he could hear his father and his wife frantically calling his name, but he ignored them. What did they know of the power that drove him on? How could they understand the harsh, wonderful, primitive power of his destiny?

Only 300 moons ago, or so the elders said, his forefathers had launched their canoes into the great unknown, casting themselves adrift on the mighty ocean, acting on faith and instinct alone, as they paddled into their future.

A journey which had brought them to this, the Big Island, and all the others that would one day be known as the Hawaii chain.

But right now, they were still being breathed into being by the gods.

And one goddess, in particular, was calling to him tonight. Born of the female spirit Haumea, or Hina, descended from Papa, the Earth Mother, and Wakea, the Sky Father.

'Pele, I hear!' he called back to the roaring molten lava gushing above him, but his voice was lost in the ominous rumblings emanating from under his feet, and the fierce winds being born in the hot, roiling air.

He staggered as the mountain heaved beneath him, but he stubbornly carried on. Below, far below, he could see the many canoes of his village fleeing into the safer embrace of Kamapuaa, the god of water.

But the man who struggled up the erupting volcano, to what seemed certain death, was listening only to the call of the woman who had invaded his dreams with her siren song.

The fire goddess.

On the other side of the mountain, great rivers of fire raced down to consume mountain, man and sea, anyone and anything that stood in its way, but unaware and uncaring, the man struggled on.

He was a sculptor by heart, a tool-maker and fisherman by trade, and as he plunged up and onwards, choking on ash and smoke, eyes running, and hearing only the roaring of his own blood, he felt his skin begin to blister.

But she wanted him. So be it. Her voice was louder than thunder, her fiery embrace sweeter than the juice of fermented fruit.

And then he fell. Cruelly, scraping his already scorched skin against needle-sharp rocks and pebbles. His legs felt weak, and he could go no further.

He began to cry, his tears drying on his face almost before they left his eyes. He would never reach her now. He was failing her. He reached out blindly, trying to haul himself up, as the ground under him shook with renewed fury. Then his hand, reaching out through the ash and smoke, grabbed something. Something hard and hot and heavy.

He lifted it towards him, bringing it close to his face in order to see it.

It was, of course, nothing more than a rock. Black rock.

The man almost threw it from him. These new islands had many such rocks. They were as numerable as the fish in the sea.

But just as his arm muscles tensed to throw it away, something stopped him. The whisper, perhaps, of the goddess herself. He looked at it again. A big black rock. Shiny. And . . . He blinked, trying desperately to wipe away tears and smoke and ash from his eyes.

Yes. He wasn't mistaken. Inside the dark density of the lava rock, he could see it. A deep glow of red. Dark red darkness of red upon darkness of red. So red it looked black. But wasn't black.

And suddenly, the sculptor knew why Pele had called him up this mountainside.

It was not to take his life, after all. Or at least, not yet.

He felt her caress all around him. Hot, fiery, unbelievably fierce. She was destruction, but she needed him.

The man rose to his feet as the erupting volcano thundered above him, and shouted his defiance and love and devotion to the darkening skies and sea wind.

His hair singed and threatened to catch fire, but he ignored it.

He waved the rock in the air, as if in defiance of all those who would defy Pele. He sang 'She-Who-Shapes-The-Sacred-Land', the most ancient of his people's chants, and laughed like a lunatic.

Perhaps all those who heard her call were driven mad. But it wouldn't stop him doing what she asked. And quickly, before he died – as he knew he soon would. Nobody could be loved by Pele, as he had been loved, and live for long.

His sculptor's tools were in a little hut on the beach by his village – but he knew both it and the village would still be standing. Pele's river of fire wouldn't touch it.

The sculptor began to run back down the hill, the rock clutched in his hand like a darkly beating, precious heart.

He had work to do. Whilst he could still see her face. . . .

Chapter One

The silver Jaguar XJS turned many heads as it roared up the motorway towards London's Heathrow airport. Not that it was going above the speed limit, for it wasn't, and its driver obviously knew how to handle it. But it was polished and gleamed to an almost glass-like intensity, and snaked expertly but safely in and out of the traffic like a line of quicksilver, catching the eye.

Behind the wheel, the driver glanced across at his passenger, wondering what was eating the kid.

Jago Marsh would have turned as many heads (nearly all of them female) as his car was doing, had he been anything other than a blur of wheat-coloured hair and dark navy Armani suit as he sped past the traffic.

'You haven't said two words since we left Windsor,' the driver remarked now, his voice a low baritone, tinged at the moment with amusement and just a shade of exasperation. 'If you're sulking about not going back to Hawaii, get over it. I told you – this is strictly business.'

Something, perhaps the ominous tone of crispness in his words, made his passenger look across at him warily.

He was a younger, softer, more compliant version of the

driver – not surprising, as Keith Marsh was Jago's only sibling.

Keith shrugged one shoulder negligently. It too was cased in Armani, but lacked his older brother's strength and width.

'Hey, I couldn't care less if I never see the place again,' he said truthfully.

Jago shot him a quick look, then glanced in the mirror, indicated, changed lanes and gears easily, and pulled away from a trundling milk tanker. The manoeuvre safely completed, he sighed heavily.

'Still got bad memories, huh?' he asked, his voice a shade more gruff now. 'Well, get over it,' he advised, not unkindly, but with an uncompromising rasp, which many of his business rivals had heard only too often. 'No woman is worth it.'

Keith sighed, thinking of Candy Mitchell, the blonde Californian who had taken him for such a ride last summer. Just how dumb could you get, Keith wondered, in a rare moment of introspection and an even rarer moment of self-disgust.

Still, she had been rich. And blonde. And had all that tanned skin and west-coast American charm which was bound to be irresistible to a young man anxious to make a reputation for himself.

A pity she was married.

'No. But sometimes—' Keith broke off and sighed wistfully. Then a cold shaft of reality intervened. He'd been lucky her husband hadn't found them out. He was almost as rich as Jago, and jealous as hell, according to Candy. He wondered if that had been half the fun for her – the danger of it all. The illicit affair with a younger man. And a Brit at that. A good-looking youngster who her husband would probably have automatically disliked heartily on sight.

'Sometimes what?' His brother's voice broke into his reverie, and Keith looked at him thoughtfully. He could never imagine Jago falling for a hard-liner like Candy. He'd chew her up for breakfast – hard as nails though she undoubtedly was. In the user stakes, it was always Jago that used.

Keith smiled ruefully. 'Nothing.'

Jago, his eyes never leaving the road, sensed his younger brother's feckless mood and scowled.

'Snap out of it,' he said curtly, the bite in his voice enough to make Keith flush.

'It's all right for you,' he snapped defensively back. 'Women never muck you around.'

Jago Marsh gave an amused bark of laughter. 'They know better. As your little princess will soon find out.'

Keith tensed. 'I thought you said this trip was purely business,' he said accusingly.

'It is,' Jago said flatly. But when Keith looked across at him, he recognized the tightly clamped jaw and the hard, tight look in his brother's profile for exactly what it was.

And felt a shiver of real unease creep up his spine.

'You're only going to buy out the Princess Mina range, yeah? That's all?' he probed, wishing he had the guts to put Jago right about what had really happened last summer. But knowing that he hadn't.

'If the deal's good enough, we'll start marketing next autumn.' But in truth, he had no real intention of giving that woman a penny of Marsh money. No matter how attractive a business deal she put on the table.

'Right,' Keith said, biting his lip. 'Just so long as you're sure it's nothing personal. That's what you always say about business, right?' he nagged, and again shot his brother a nervous look.

15

He didn't like the look of that hard profile one little bit. He wished, now, that he'd just kept his mouth shut all those months ago. The only trouble was, once you'd told one lie, it snowballed. Growing and growing into something monstrous which could flatten you.

Or in this case, flatten someone else.

'That's right,' Jago agreed. 'Business is one thing. Everything else is another.' It was, Jago thought wryly, a hard motto, but one which bitter experience over the years had taught him held only too true.

Keith sighed. 'Well, you should know,' he said flatly, making his brother take his eyes off the road for just a split second, to give him a quick, all-seeing glance.

Had Keith been looking at him, he would have found the familiar, steely-grey eyes going right through him. Jago had always been able to read him like a book.

At thirty-three he was nearly a full ten years older than Keith, and by the time Keith started attending primary school, his older brother had already possessed a wise and uncompromising view of the world, and human nature, that went far beyond his tender years.

Not that he'd been allowed many tender years on the Bordman estate, the tough, crime-ridden high-rise flats where the Marsh boys had grown up.

Their father had left shortly after Keith's birth, too lazy or too afraid to contemplate life with another hungry mouth to feed. By the time half of his Social Security money had gone on bottles of whisky, there was even less left to stretch between them.

His mother hadn't been all that sorry to see him go, if the truth be told. With him out of the way, she'd been able to convert their tiny bedroom into an extra workspace, where

16

she took on the mind-numbingly dull job of envelope-packing to make ends meet.

Once Keith had started school, she was able to get out of the dingy high-rise flat and take on a part-time job. What with that, and doing cleaning work late at nights and early in the mornings, she was able to afford even the odd pair of trainers for her eldest child, who seemed to grow taller and harder by the day.

Not that Jago wasn't already adding to the family budget himself by then. He had his own early-morning paper round, plus working the few hours government child labour restrictions allowed, in a grocery store run by a beleaguered Pakistani couple just off the estate.

Twice he'd been present during a robbery, once taking on the robbers and earning himself a glass bottle thrust into his face for his pains.

Despite the blood flowing into his eyes and temporarily blinding him, he'd held on to one robber, whilst the other had fled empty-handed. The shop owner had been ecstatic, and given him an immediate raise, but the police, though impressed, had warned him that 'having a go' wasn't a good policy.

Nevertheless, the shop wasn't raided again, until after Jago stopped working there.

It wasn't surprising to Keith, therefore, that Jago was always someone to be treated with respect. Even the ever-present drug dealers, constantly to be found lurking in garages and under overpasses around the estate, gave him a wide berth. The wicked scar on his face, plus his reputation as someone not to be messed with, grew in proportion to his height and nous, and was the main reason that Keith was never opportuned by those who regularly preyed on school children.

Jago had left school at sixteen, much to his mother's dismay, who'd always thought her eldest son had by far the best brains of anyone in the family – hers or her erstwhile husband's. But, in spite of his impressive exam results, she'd acknowledged the truth of his argument that earning money had to take priority. Keith was growing up and needed clothes, the rent was always being demanded, and the price of living was an ever-heavy, ponderous weight, making their mother old before her time.

So Jago had gone straight into a job at a local factory – a medical equipment supply factory. Even now, years later, Keith still had vivid memories of him coming home to the flat and stowing away his equipment – gloves of a hard-wearing stiffened material for when he was packing needles, white overalls which always smelled of some kind of disinfectant, and boxes of silly little paper shoes which he had to wear over his own.

He'd never seemed tired, though. Never defeated or worn down, as he'd seen so many other men.

'Earth to planet Keith. Come in, Keith.'

Keith grinned. 'I hear you.'

'Thought you'd gone off to join the Star Trek team for a minute there,' Jago teased.

'Nope. Just thinking.'

'About her? The princess? Forget her. Charis Scott isn't worth a moment's thought,' Jago said grimly, and Keith almost jumped.

Charis Scott? He hadn't thought about Charis in months. It always gave him a wriggling feeling of embarrassed shame whenever he did so, so he'd stopped doing it. As simple as that. Now, though, all his lies were coming back to haunt him, and all his fears about Jago's up-coming trip to Hawaii came rushing back in an ominous flood of foreboding.

'Charis is all right,' he said uneasily. 'Jago, you're not going to do anything . . . unpleasant, are you?' he asked nervously.

He watched his brother smile. And it sent shivers down his spine.

'Of course not,' Jago said softly.

Keith bit his lip and turned away, cursing himself anew. Why the hell hadn't he kept his mouth shut about Charis?

But he knew the answer to that all right.

When he'd come back from Hawaii last year, Jago had taken one look at him and asked straight out why he'd looked like a whipped dog.

And Keith had thought he'd pulled off his homecoming really well. His mother, Diane, had met him at the airport in the sporty new model Jago had got her for Christmas, and she hadn't noticed anything wrong. Keith was rather proud of the way he'd shown off his tan and regaled her with hilarious stories of tourists and the rumbling volcanoes of the Big Island.

If his own mother hadn't twigged to the fact that he felt sick and stupid and humiliated and angry at himself, why had Jago?

Silly question, Keith realized immediately.

Jago always knew.

The moment he'd walked into the big house on the outskirts of Windsor (the first personal purchase Jago had made after making his first million), Jago had read him like a book.

Waiting until Diane had left for the evening to go to an amateur dramatics society meeting, he'd wasted no time in tackling him.

What chance had he really had?

Jago had been relentless. Was it money? He'd gone over to

the islands ostensibly on a business trip and fact-finding mission. Ever since he'd started work as a junior executive at Marsh Pharmaceuticals, Jago had been giving him gradually increasing responsibilities, teaching him the business slowly, always monitoring him and making sure he never got out of his depth.

Had he put too much pressure on him?

No, Keith had assured him, he hadn't lost any precious money. The banks he'd been asked to check out, the exchange rate systems he'd been told to look into, the market explorations Jago had set out, had all been seen to. He hadn't been lured into any get-rich-quick schemes from voracious American businessmen. He could read the reports in the morning. His secretary had them all typed up.

Jago had grunted, then nodded, his eyes narrowing suspiciously. 'Then it's got to be a woman,' he'd said flatly.

And Keith hadn't been able to deny it. Or at least, not with any credibility.

But there was no way he was going to admit to his big brother – the whizz-kid, millionaire, rags-to-riches, hard-as-nails, take-no-prisoners darling of the English big business world – that he'd just spent two months as the toy-boy plaything of a bored Californian piranah named Candy, only to then be tossed aside for a French casino owner's son with a new speedboat.

He'd rather die.

Now, as they pulled into one of Heathrow's many car parks, he could almost wish he had.

For the lies he'd told Jago instead, just to get him off his back and let him nurse his wounded pride and spirit in peace, had been, in their own way, even worse than the truth.

Perhaps he should call Charis up and warn her about Jago?

For all his talk about things being strictly business, he knew when his brother was on the warpath. It would be the least, the very least, he could do to give her a heads-up. But that was even supposing he could get her to take his calls in the first place. After what had happened last summer, he doubted she'd ever want to talk to him again.

And why should she? He'd been a creep of the first order. Even now, he burned with shame whenever he thought about it.

'You going to see me off, or can't you wait to get behind the wheel?' Jago asked, unhooking the seatbelt and glancing across at Keith, again with that indulgent smile, tinged with exasperation, playing with the firm line of his lips.

'I'm not a kid any more,' Keith said, caught on the raw as always. Living in a big brother's shadow got real stale, real fast. And it didn't help when he was so damned protective and, well, *good to you*, all the time, either. 'I have been driving since I was seventeen. And I've got my own motor,' he added, appalled at the petulance in his voice.

'OK, OK, don't bite my head off.' Jago grinned, but his grey eyes were dark and steady.

He was still hurting, that was obvious, Jago thought grimly. That damned woman had really done a job on him.

Still, she was soon going to learn that you didn't mess with a Marsh and get away with it.

Those days were over. Life might have had the upper hand of him and his family once, but he'd long since got a stranglehold on it, and wasn't about to let go now.

As they walked into the terminal, located the right gate, checked in his luggage and went on to the VIP lounge to wait for the flight to be called, Jago's mind also winged back to the bad old days.

He'd worked extra shifts in the factory almost from the first time he'd been eligible to get overtime. At first it had been purely for the money. Then later, as he began to learn more about the factory, what it produced, where it went, and the good it did, he became more and more fascinated in the products themselves.

Inevitably, he'd caught the eye of one of the factory's foremen. His quick intelligence soon had him promoted. Night classes in management and economics and business practise quickly followed.

Then, over a five-year period, a rise to executive status. The friends he'd made on the factory floor, inevitably, and with real regret on his part, fell by the wayside as he transmogrified from one of 'us' to one of 'them'.

All in all, he'd spent over seven years at the factory, doing everything from packing surgical swabs in boxes to ordering hundreds of thousands of pounds' worth of state-of-the-art medical equipment, from pacemakers to artificial limbs. He'd travelled the world on business, learned to read balance sheets as easily as the written word, worked like a dog and absorbed information like a sponge.

And then he'd left.

Everyone had thought that he was mad – including his mother. They'd been able to leave the hellish confines of the Bordman estate to a modest semi in a nearby neighbourhood, thanks to Jago's rising fortunes.

Why, his mother had asked, did he want to leave a job where he wore a smart suit to work, drove a company car, got to travel abroad regularly, and clearly had good promotion prospects ahead of him? With his savvy, he could climb the ladder as high as he wanted to go.

But Jago didn't want to climb somebody else's ladder; he

wanted to make his own. And had.

With a loan from the bank, all but seduced from an impressed (and rather smitten) female loans advisor, he'd started Marsh Pharmaceuticals.

It hadn't exactly created waves, and caused no panic or even notice from anybody at all. It had a small workforce, operated out of a big warehouse in a rundown section by the river. It turned out standard fare – bandages, plasters, thermometers, blood-pressure gauges, and all the usual bread-and-butter equipment associated with the medical profession.

And then it started to employ more. It won larger and bigger contracts. Its chairman and sole owner, Jago Marsh, began to become known in the 'city' as a tough negotiator. He could undercut ruthlessly. He could swim with even the biggest sharks, somehow always managing not to get huge chunks bitten out of his own flanks, whilst feeding well himself.

He bought up surrounding warehouses, dirt cheap, and expanded. The area changed, became more upmarket, and he sold out to a consortium interested in creating Yuppie riverside housing for a huge profit. From there he bought a factory in a prestigious industrial estate and moved into more sophisticated machinery. The meters which diabetics used to take daily blood sugar/glucose readings. Pacemakers. Surgical implants. He employed only the best technicians, engineers, designers and graduates, not only from London's best technical colleges but from abroad as well, particularly America's Ivy League players.

Within five years, he was a multi-millionaire, his company regularly making profits which would have made him ripe for a take-over had he ever gone public, which he never had, despite all the inducements. Which was what made Marsh Pharmaceuticals today one of the biggest privately owned companies of its kind in the UK.

'Gate seven,' Keith said, making Jago glance up from the *Financial Times* he wasn't reading.

'What?'

'Your flight. It's being called at gate seven. And you accuse me of daydreaming,' Keith teased, delighted to find this rare opportunity to catch his brother napping.

Jago grinned and pointed a long bony finger at him. 'Watch it. Now don't forget, the Nagatashi meeting on Wednesday. Don't go above five point six million, no matter what. The assets alone won't cover that, and they know it.'

'Yeah, yeah, I know. You are only on the end of a phone, you know. Hawaii isn't the end of the world – it just feels like it.'

He laughed and dodged the fake punch Jago sent his way.

They walked through the crowds amicably together, but as they neared the gate, Keith again fell to biting his lip and feeling uneasy. It was no good. He just had to try and do something.

'Jago, about Charis,' he said tentatively. 'She's all right, you know? I mean . . .' He faltered as the steely grey eyes fastened on his. 'It's not all her fault,' he finished feebly, wincing internally as he did so. Actually, he mentally added, none of it was her fault, but in the face of his brother's flat, assessing gaze, found the words drying up in his throat.

'Stop worrying about your little princess,' Jago said tightly. 'I'll take care of her.'

'That's what worries me,' Keith flashed, then quickly looked away as Jago's eyes narrowed.

'Is there something else, something that you haven't told me about?' Jago asked, his voice a low, ominous rumble which reminded Keith of Hawaii's volcanoes. And just like those magical, awe-inspiring mountains, Keith knew that Jago was more than capable of spitting fire himself, on occasion.

'No, of course not,' he said, cursing himself for his chicken-heartedness, just as he cursed himself for his childish optimism, which always came to his rescue during moments of crisis.

But maybe things *would* be all right. After all, from what he remembered of Charis Scott, she'd be more than capable of taking care of herself. Maybe she'd even give Jago a run for his money.

Yeah. Maybe.

Or maybe he was worrying about nothing. Maybe Jago really was just flying out to Hawaii on a business deal. Even if the Princess Mina range was hardly the sort of thing he'd have thought Marsh Pharmaceuticals to be interested in.

Jago watched the misery come and go in his brother's face, recognizing his expressions of angst but totally misreading their source, and felt a grim fury gnaw at his innards.

Ever since his father had left, he'd always known it was up to him to take care of things. To look after Diane, make sure Keith didn't have to leave school at sixteen as he had, but get a decent education, and generally be the man of the house-hold.

It had been up to him to get them out of Bordman estate and into somewhere decent. Up to him to see that the Marsh family not only survived but prospered.

As it had.

Diane had long since lost that haggard, old-before-her-time look, and now dressed in Yves St Laurent and wore Paloma Picasso perfume. Keith had been to Windsor School, then Durham.

So ingrained in him was it that he had to protect them, that when Keith had come back from Hawaii, mangled and torn from what that harridan Charis Scott had done to him, he'd hardly even had to make a conscious decision to do something about it.

No matter how long it took.

And now, the time was here. He'd known it was, the moment the grapevine had told him she was selling her Princess Mina range.

Keith seemed to be well on the way to getting over her, although he didn't like the way he kept defending her, and business was quiet. He hadn't had a holiday in years. And there was one other little matter he hadn't told Keith about, which had made him finally decide to schedule this trip to the Big Island.

Yes, all in all, Jago Marsh was looking forward to this trip. He expected to get good things out of it.

The final call came over the com system, and Jago gave Keith a brief slap on the back, issuing more last-minute instructions about the rest of the month's business meetings and schedules. Not that he wasn't taking his PC, and could be hooked up to the office and his secretary (always super-efficient) by the time you could say videocom uplink.

If necessary, Jago knew that he could run the firm from Hawaii itself. Not that it wouldn't do Keith good to have a taste of real responsibility for a bit.

After being knocked back by a woman, a man's ego needed something to give it a boost.

He should know.

Not that he'd thought of Robyn in years.

On board the big jet, he was quickly shown into first class by a pretty stewardess with bobbed black hair and big blue

Irish eyes. He accepted a glass of champagne from her whilst they awaited taxiing and clearance, and tried to recall what Robyn looked like.

It seemed so long ago – another lifetime, in fact – that all he got was impressions. Glossy hair, a hard, well-maintained façade. A cutting upper-class accent. The once-rich daddy.

He should have known better.

Why else would a Sloane Ranger marry a scarred, working-class boy from Bordmans, unless he was stinking rich?

Answer.

She wouldn't.

Lucky for him, though, he'd overheard her talking to her friends one day, laughing scornfully at his choice of engagement ring, and assuring them that she'd soon teach him some class. And, so she'd informed them blithely, once she was divorced, with a nice alimony settlement in the bank, she'd spread some of his wealth back their way. Promise, sweeties.

Their combined laughter had been enough to take the enamel off his teeth.

Well, Jago had, he thought, broken off their engagement with a great deal of class.

At least he thought so.

Now his clearest memory of Robyn was her mouth falling open in surprise as he'd taken the engagement ring off her finger, telling her just what he truly thought of her daddy into the bargain.

'Would you like some more champagne, sir, after we're airborne?' A lilting Irish voice had his mind snapping back to the here and now.

'No, thanks. One is enough,' he said with a smile. In truth, although he could afford the best champagne in the world (or even buy one of the best vineyards), he rarely drank. He had smoked, for a brief period in his youth, but had quit cold turkey when he'd first become aware of the health problems associated with it.

He sat back in his seat as the big powerful engines turned, looking out of the window as the runway sped by, and then smiling slightly as he felt the massive machine lift off the ground.

So he was on his way to Hawaii.

Flying was nothing new to him, of course. He regularly flew to the states and Europe, in the cause of making Marsh Pharmaceuticals the biggest and best in the world.

But this was different.

This was a holiday. Of sorts.

And payback time.

And, of course, an opportunity to revel in his one true indulgence.

Like a lot of self-made men, Jago knew he lacked many things which a more well-rounded, cosmopolitanly educated man might lack.

Which perhaps explained what he thought of as his only idiosyncrasy.

His collection of Polynesian art.

He wasn't sure what had started it all off. A Gauguin painting, which he'd bought strictly as an investment, perhaps. Followed by a piece of pottery, associated with the island in the painting. Then a statue. And suddenly he found he was reading books on the subject. Trawling papers for records of sales. Travelling miles out of his way to attend auctions.

And before he knew it, he was hooked. He was a collector. And, moreover, one with enough money and natural taste to collect only the best of their kind.

'Menu, sir?' The same lilting Irish voice once again brought him back to reality, and he accepted the laminated card from her with a vague smile.

The stewardess, whose name tag labelled her as Maureen O'Riley, returned to the stewardesses' station and grinned at her friend. 'Wow,' she said briefly but descriptively.

'Swap you seats,' Inga Svensen said teasingly, and Maureen laughed.

'Not on your sweet life. Have you taken a good look at him?'

Inga had. Coming from a land of fair-haired men, she hadn't paid much attention when her friend Maureen had told her they had an Adonis on board, their code word for a real hunk.

She'd glanced down into first class, seen a wheat-blond head, gauged from the amount of seat he took up that he was at least six feet tall, with broad shoulders, and made a mental note to check him out next time she went past.

And was she glad she had.

Maureen was right.

He was gorgeous. With a high forehead, thin but distinctive nose, firm-lipped mouth and strongly moulded chin, he was aggressively handsome rather than masculinely beautiful. And the pale, jagged scar, running from the bottom left-hand corner of his right eye down to the side of his cheek, only emphasized the rather dangerous aura which hung about him.

He was the kind of man that made you worry as well as dream. You sensed his power. He looked hard, and even his eyes were the colour of steel. Yet you sensed something warm under the hardness. Something exciting. Something worth taking the risk of getting hurt for.

Jago, unaware of the speculation of the two stewardesses, leaned forward and withdrew two folders from his briefcase.

One was a personal history of Charis Mina Scott, and her Princess Mina range of beauty products, but although he hesitated over it, he left it unopened.

He'd already studied it in depth, and knew all about her royal highness, and her illustrious family and chi-chi little company.

He'd deal with her later. And with a great deal of pleasure.

So she thought she could rub a Marsh into the dust and get away with it, did she? She'd soon learn better. Keith, no doubt, had been young and foolish and ripe for a fall, a fact she'd probably realized from the first moment they'd met. But let her take on *big* brother, and see how she fared then!

Although there was no picture of Charis Scott in the file, from what Keith had said, she was a typical Hawaiian beauty. With her title and money she no doubt thought she was quite something. She probably wasn't even surprised when Marsh Pharmaceuticals, a world giant, had offered to buy her out.

No doubt she had taken it as no more than her due. But let her preen.

She would soon learn that she had nothing he really wanted. Not her oh-so-prolific charms, or her pathetic little business.

No, that was not quite right.

She *did* have *one* thing that he wanted. And it was something that he was going to acquire for himself, come hell or high water.

So thinking, he opened the second folder, and gazed down with a collector's zeal at the photograph of the object pictured.

Now *she* was a *real* Hawaiian beauty.

And she was going to be his.

Chapter Two

Hawaii

The battered Jeep rocked from side to side on badly adjusted shock absorbers as it climbed a steep incline on Saddle Road, the sometimes hazardous trail which cut a straight line, east to west, across the Big Island, otherwise known as Hawaii.

Naomi Bridges looked up from the portable PC on her lap, currently relaying the latest seismograph readings from her lab at the Hawaiian Volcano Observatory. She frowned over the figures relating to the small tremors which had been recorded yesterday morning, wondering what it was about them that had worried Riordan so much. They didn't look in any way out of the ordinary to her. But then she was not one of the world's most respected volcanologists.

'There have been no more tremors since 5.42 a.m., yesterday,' she remarked, glancing up as they passed through Kipuka Puaulu Bird Sanctuary.

Dr Riordan Vane, visiting Chief scientist, attached to the observatory for two years, frowned and shook his head, but said nothing.

Turning north, he left the relatively well-paved surface of

Saddle Road for the dirt track, pitted and strewn with volcanic rock, which led to Mount Kulahaleha, the Big Island's smallest active volcano.

He had chosen to study this volcano, rather than the more spectacular Mauna Loa, Mauna Kea or even Kilauea, mostly because of the unusual seismographic and tiltmeter readings that had been coming from the mountain during the last few years.

Now he pulled the Jeep to a halt at the end of the trail and switched off the engine.

He glanced at his assistant, who was already tightening the laces on her sturdy hiking boots, and smiled fleetingly.

'Think we're on to a wild goose chase?' he asked lightly.

Naomi looked up, her short, pale blonde hair already darkening in the humidity and heat. Although Hawaii had much the same temperature all the year round, in June the humidity levels could sky-rocket. Usually, though, a trade wind helped her keep her cool.

She smiled, her pale blue eyes crinkling attractively.

'Not me. I have perfect faith in your predictions.' It was, she thought wryly, a pity that the other volcanologists at the institute back home, and here at the observatory, didn't feel the same way.

Riordan shook his head. 'Anybody ever tell you you're too gullible for words?' he asked amicably.

Naomi laughed unrestrainedly. 'No, I can't say they ever have.'

For they'd never had reason to. Naïve she was not, and never had been.

She'd been born and raised in Portsmouth, of a large, down-to-earth family, where she'd attended the local college before getting a scholarship and moving to London to do a postgraduate degree course in the hardly female-orientated sphere of volcanology.

Not brilliant, but by no means one of those who had to struggle, she'd been granted her doctorate and had been lucky enough to secure a post in Sicily, on Dr Vane's team.

It had taken him, Naomi supposed wryly, about two and a half years to know her face, and another year after that to remember her name. Unlike the subjects she studied with such fascinated diligence, she was not, it seemed, the type to set the world on fire. And certainly not the type to set Dr Vane's blood boiling.

She glanced determinedly away from him as he got out of the Jeep, studiously avoiding the sight of his strong, tanned thighs, encased only in workmanlike denim shorts, as he planted his feet firmly on the dark volcanic rock which littered this part of the world. Unlike herself, he looked as cool as a cucumber, as at home on the slopes of a volcano as some men were in an air-conditioned office.

All around her, lush green forests of koa trees, pandanus and the native ohia lehua crowded, like pushy neighbours, up the sides of the mountain. Only at the middle elevation did the rock-and-shrub-strewn landscape, indicating an active volcano at work, take over.

Overhead a flock of birds, as yet unknown to her, flew noisily overhead. Naomi and Riordan had only come to the Big Island that January, and had been so busy she'd had little time for sight-seeing or getting to know the locals – be they feathered or two-legged.

She hoisted out a huge and heavy backpack, hardly noticing its bulk or weight any more, she'd become so used to lugging it about over the past years. It had kept her fit and strong – being better than ten aerobic classes put together.

As she slipped it on over her shoulders, her eyes scanned towards the north-east, where the silversword plant, native only to the islands, gave way to the more prolific cane fields and coconut groves.

'All set?' Riordan's voice had her swinging her neat little head around. Although she'd acquired something of a tan since coming here – it was hard to avoid – she was nowhere near as nut-brown and healthy-looking as her boss.

Perhaps it was his colouring. With a somewhat carelessly cut head of brown hair, thick dark brows over surprisingly blue eyes, he was as tanned as any Polynesian. His own rucksack weighed probably twice what hers did, packed as it was with instrumentation, but he too hefted it on to his back as if it were packed with swansdown.

She smiled brightly. 'Just lead the way, chief,' she responded cheerfully.

She'd been lucky, she knew, to be picked to be his right-hand man on this assignment, and had beaten several others to the job, amongst much mumbling and rumblings. But she'd worked with Dr Vane for over seven years now, doing good and steady work, and wasn't about to let her detractors convince her that she hadn't deserved, or earned, this job.

They began to trek upwards, towards the crater and slightly to the west, to where the first of the tiltmeter stations were placed.

She knew several teams from the labs had been up that morning, setting them up, and had already taken readings. She wasn't sure, therefore, what they were doing retracing their steps but she wasn't about to question Riordan. He knew what he was doing.

Amongst his field, he was, without doubt, one of the most eminent. And if this otherwise undistinguished volcano had caught his eye, there was sure to be a good reason for it. For, out of all his contemporaries, venerable and mega-experienced men of science though they were, it was Riordan who'd constantly had the most success at predicting eruptions. Sometimes Naomi wondered if he and the mighty mountains had some kind of psychic link, so uncanny was his affinity with them.

It was nearly an hour of hard trekking before they reached the first station, and it was just as well, Naomi thought for the thousandth time during one of these expeditions, that she'd inherited her wiry build from her father. One of those annoying women who could eat like a horse but never put on weight, her five-foot ten-inch frame was as lean and as malleable as willow.

Ahead of her, Riordan reached into one of the pockets of the rucksack and brought out a water bottle. It was easy, she knew, to become dehydrated when working. Not only was the climate hard on those used to more northern temperatures, but the air was thinner up here, and the work physically laborious.

She smiled as he first handed it to her. The gesture was typical of the man. Courteous, unthinking and practical. In all the years she'd known him, she'd never heard him swear, never seen him drunk, and never heard him talk about himself.

All she'd learned about him had been culled from other people, chance remarks and luck.

She took a drink, relishing even the slightly warm mineral water, then handed it back. She watched as he tipped his head back, his Adam's apple bobbing as he swallowed strongly. When he straightened, she was looking firmly upwards, towards the rim of the volcano.

35

'Looks peaceful, doesn't it?' he remarked thoughtfully, as indeed it did.

The sky above the crater rim was cerulean blue, with only a few wispy white clouds for company. For once, visibility was ideal, with no mist or rain-clouds to mar the view. A light trade wind blew dust in lazy swirls. Not a plume of smoke or a cough of ash issued from the bowels of the mountain.

It was, in fact, very hard to imagine this volcano spewing out rivers of molten rock – though it had once, and only just over twenty-five years ago.

'But I'll bet you last month's budget that the tiltmeters show movement,' he added, his voice almost wistful.

Naomi wasn't about to take that bet. She knew better than to second-guess Riordan Vane in anything.

Although some grad students from the observatory had already taken the readings, neither Naomi or Riordan had yet seen them, as they'd headed straight here from their temporary digs in Hilo.

They walked on, coming across the first tiltmeter. The grad students had left it set up, knowing that Dr Vane was going to personally inspect it later on, though usually they were assembled, checked, then disassembled and taken on to the next station.

That would have to wait, however. Riordan had specifically asked that this station be left intact. Without being asked, Naomi set to work, unpacking the gauges, meters, measuring devices, thermometers and other paraphernalia which was a part of her everyday life.

She watched Riordan measuring the tiltmeters, standing by ready with her notebook to make recordings.

Unlike seismograph stations, which automatically and constantly sent data back to the monitors at the lab, tiltmeter readings were still done the old-fashioned way.

To a layman, the station was comprised of three concrete piers, about three feet high, and firmly anchored in bedrock. Small pots, about the size of saucepans, were filled with water and attached with hoses. By this incredibly simple method, the water levels in each pier could be monitored, measured and recorded, to check on any ground swells. Water, always running off to the lowest level, would make sure of that.

For, as Naomi knew only too well, a volcano actually became swollen when the magma chamber began to fill. The ground, too, could become warm, making the science of volcanology sometimes incredibly simple but also incredibly complicated – as anyone watching them for the next few hours would certainly testify.

Naomi, used to instruments of both amazing sensitivity and complexity, found nothing extraordinary in what she was doing, however.

Eventually, with the afternoon sun beaming down relentlessly, they began to pack away. As usual, Riordan had forgotten about lunch, and Naomi's tummy began to rumble its discontent. But there would be no stopping at a roadside café on the way back to the observatory, that she would have bet money on, for Riordan was anxious to put on his mathematicians' cap and get the readings analyzed.

Back at the observatory, Naomi dropped her boss off then took the Jeep to Volcano House Hotel, for a well-earned treat. It wasn't often that she ate at the prestigious hotel, and it was a sign of the staff's esteem for volcanologists that nobody raised an eyebrow at her rather dusty, sweat-stained khaki blouse and multi-pocketed, hard-wearing shorts in the same uninspiring colour.

She took a seat in a café with a panoramic view over the

volcano, and sighed in bliss as the waiter brought her the Kona coffee she ordered.

'*Mahalo,*' she murmured, thanking him, and getting a big flashing smile in return. She assumed it was because she'd taken the trouble to learn a little of the native language, and would probably have been surprised to learn that her voice had very little to do with the waiter's appreciation.

Even dressed as she was, Naomi's pale colouring, slender figure and warm smile would always win her approval.

She glanced at the menu, grimacing at some of the pricier but delicious delicacies on offer. In the end, she opted for a tropical platter, consisting of crabmeat, avocado, chopped macadamia nuts, grapefruit, lettuce and lemon dressing. For dessert, she had the ever-popular haupia, a coconut pudding which tasted wonderful.

Trying not to feel guilty about Riordan, slaving over a hot monitor and tables of figures back at the lab, she ordered another Kona coffee and looked out over the impressive view that had visitors from all over the world flocking to the hotel.

The crater was breathtaking. Compared to their own modest volcano, Kilauea was a monster.

She listened vaguely to the chatter of the excited guests and tourists all around her, some talking with awe about the beauty of the sight in front of them, whilst others told horror stories about eruptions. She wondered what they'd say if she told them she studied active volcanoes for a living.

'Well, as I live and breathe, if it isn't the gorgeous Dr Bridges! What brings you into the realm of us mere plebs?'

Naomi felt herself grinning as the familiar drawl of Danny Okala, one of the *Hawaiian Herald*'s finest reporters (according to Danny), filled the air above her. She craned her neck backwards, getting a somewhat kaleidoscopic view of brightly patterned shirt and oily dark hair, and held up her hand.

It was lightly slapped.

'Danny, just the man. I was thinking of going back to work and I desperately need someone to lead me astray,' she greeted him cheerfully. They'd met when Danny had been assigned to the story of Dr Vane's two-year secondment to Hawaii, and he'd hastily fobbed the reporter off on to her.

Danny grinned wolfishly and slipped into the seat beside her. 'In that case, my dear *nani wahini*, I'm definitely the man for you,' he assured her, dark eyes twinkling.

He was about fifty, fat, and very happily married, and had more children than even his wife knew about, or so the locals would have it.

Naomi looked at him suspiciously. 'What did you just call me?' she asked. Her Hawaiian wasn't that far advanced just yet.

Danny held up a hand in appeasement. 'I called you my beautiful girl. I swear!' he said solemnly, then spoiled it by grinning widely and ordering an okolehao, the infamous local brew made from some kind of root. It almost seemed to take out your teeth by the roots too, as Naomi recalled. She'd only tried it the once, and after her first sip of it, had vowed never again.

She shuddered as she watched him drink with obvious pleasure.

'But why on earth would you be thinking of going back to that grim underground lab, when you can be out on a day like this?' Danny waved eloquently at the view outside. 'Or has that slave-driver you call a boss been checking up on you?'

Naomi laughed. 'No, he hasn't, and he isn't a slave-driver.'

Danny looked at her sceptically. 'No? You could have fooled me. I spent nearly all day with you when I did that piece,

39

remember? And from what I can recall, you worked even longer hours than me.'

Naomi laughed. 'Danny, you don't work at all!'

'True. But I'm always on duty. Take right now, for instance. To you, it may look as if I'm squandering away the afternoon, drinking and hob-nobbing with the hoi polloi. Really, I'm on the look-out for a celeb which, rumour has it, is shacked up here on the QT.' He leaned forward and named a well-known Hollywood heart-throb, who Naomi had only vaguely heard of, and a supermodel. 'And I'm here with my trusty hidden camera' – he waved one loose-fitting sleeve about vaguely, which did indeed look as if it had something concealed up it, and nodded knowingly – 'waiting to pounce. It's a lousy job but somebody yada-yada-yada.' He waved his hand about like a world-weary pantomime dame and drank his drink sorrow-fully.

Naomi grinned and shook her head. 'Poor you. And for your information, Riordan doesn't realize how much time he's putting in himself, so he doesn't realize how much he asks of his assistants. Not that I mind, anyway. The work is fascinating.'

Danny's old and wise eyes twinkled. 'Soft on him, ain't ya?' he said devastatingly, and as Naomi gaped and gulped, ordered another drink.

'Don't be ridiculous,' Naomi finally spluttered, her face a little paler under her tan. Something, perhaps a touch of real fear in the depths of her pale blue eyes, had the reporter's smile falling away.

'Look, it's none of my business. Honest,' Danny said placat-ingly. 'But what's stopping you? The man's available, isn't he? Last I heard, he was a widow of some years standing. Why don't you go for it, *wahini*? You young things nowadays don't need to wait to be asked, after all.'

Naomi dipped her face towards her coffee cup and took a sip, desperately trying to gather her wits.

Was it that obvious? She thought she'd kept her feelings for Riordan Vane well and truly under wraps. In a close-knit community, as the scientific world often was, there wasn't even a hint of a whisper about Riordan and herself, of that she was sure. And gossip travelled even faster than seismic shocks.

But then why should there be rumours? As far as Riordan was concerned, she was practically just another piece of equipment. And as for how she felt about him. . . . Well, she was certain she'd kept that from showing, even from her best friend and her family.

She even dated other men, for Pete's sake.

True, not for long. And it never got to the physical stage. But even so, she was sure, nobody, nobody at all, had picked up even the merest hint that she'd been in love with her boss almost from the first moment she'd met him.

And why should they?

At first, even she hadn't known it herself. She'd been over-awed to be working with the great man himself, and had thrown herself into her work, determined not to let him down or regret hiring her. Then, over the years, as hero worship had turned to respect, then admiration, then love, and she'd become aware of the true nature of her feelings, she'd become ultra careful about her behaviour.

On the rare occasions that Riordan and his team went out for a drink, or held a Christmas party, or a post-eruption cele-bration, she was always careful to be 'just one of the guys', being neither too friendly nor too stand-offish with the big boss. She never let herself gaze at him, though sometimes, when they were strictly alone, she did indulge herself in this illlicit pastime. She never dressed in anything other than the usual working uniform of shirts, shorts or slacks. She never talked about personal topics.

No, she was sure, nobody knew her secret. Until this man, this cheerful, easy-going reporter, just dropped his bombshell.

She had to diffuse it. And quick.

'Danny, when you told me you were an incurable romantic, I never thought you actually meant it. Now, though, I can see you were right,' she drawled.

Danny rolled his eyes. 'Uh-huh. Tell it to the tooth fairy. Anyone can see you were made for each other. Though' – and here he left off to scratch his unshaven chin, the rasping sound setting her nerves on edge – 'it's obvious that the man himself is woefully blind to the fact. Tell me, does he do nothing but think of mountains?'

'Sure he does,' Naomi laughed, determined to lighten the mood and steer him on to less dangerous territory. 'He thinks about magnetic anomalies, eruptive rift zones and gas samples. Just as I do,' she added firmly. 'It's our job, Danny. Some of us still do work for a living, you know.'

Danny clutched his heart. 'You wound me. And don't think you've succeeded in distracting me, either.' He made her heart sink by wagging a finger at her. 'We were talking about your love life, which is far more interesting than even volcanoes. Now, just what is the problem, my pet? The good doctor must be made of iron not to notice you. So what's the trouble? He like redheads or what? If so,' and here the incorrigible rogue began to chuckle wickedly, 'I suggest you invest in a bottle of hair dye.'

Naomi didn't know whether to laugh or cry. But really, it was absurd. In this day and age, to suffer from unrequited love did seem rather dramatic of her. It would be funny, if only it didn't hurt so!

'Danny, let's just forget it, hmm? Dr Vane and I are colleagues and that's all. I haven't ever given him any reason to notice me, and besides all that . . . He's still in mourning for his wife.'

There. She'd said it.

Danny cocked his head to one side, and pondered. 'But hasn't it been over five years since she died? A car accident, wasn't it?'

'Yes,' Naomi snapped. 'And *he* was driving. Now can we please change the subject?'

'Ah,' Danny said, his sunny face becoming serious. 'Yes. That's bad. Guilt can do serious damage to a man's soul. Now I begin to understand him better. I thought he was just cold. And perhaps a little obsessed with Madam Pele, yes? Now I understand better.' He gave Naomi a kindly look, which had her cringing inside. 'You didn't pick an easy man to love, did you, my *nani* one? Oh, and speaking of the goddess herself, did you know she'd been spotted?'

Naomi blinked, trying to keep up with his change of mood, and pretending that none of his words had caught her on the raw.

'Who? Pele? She's the goddess of volcanoes, isn't she?' she asked. Like the Hawaiian language, she was slowly learning something of the Big Island's mythology too.

'That's right. According to the old ones, Pele is always seen before an eruption.' And here Danny nodded his head wisely, the contemporary, slightly world-weary reporter being momentarily overtaken by a far more thoughtful and pagan self.

'Yes, she's been seen at least three times. By old Auntie Kama, and two old-timers up at the polo field. They were in their groundsman's hut when it happened.'

And again he nodded. There was something so wise and knowing about the look on his face. In spite of herself, Naomi felt a cold frisson of fear snake up her spine.

Then she shrugged it off. Well, at least they weren't talking about her doomed feelings for Riordan any more.

'You do talk a lot of guff, Danny,' she said. 'They probably saw one of those lovely young dancers, all dressed up to do a hula show at one of the resorts.'

'Ha, now you show your ignorance,' Danny said, but not unkindly. 'She always appears as a very old woman before an eruption, not as a lovely young thing. She had long white hair, and is dressed in white.'

'Well, if you say so,' Naomi said. And wondered. First Riordan seemed sure that Kulahaleha was about to blow, and now there seemed to be some local groundswell of feelings (true, granted on superstition), which nevertheless amounted to the same belief.

But she was a woman of science, and so shrugged. 'Anyway, much as I'd like to sit and discuss Madam Pele with you, I have to get back. Riordan's probably finished analyzing the tiltmeter readings by now.'

And now, more than ever, she was anxious to see what they were. She couldn't help the feeling of tingling excitement she got whenever she contemplated an eruption. Although she'd been present at only two eruptions during her career, and neither one of them major, it was impossible to become blasé at the thought of another.

She only hoped, if an eruption occurred, that people would be evacuated in time. Not that there were any big towns or even small villages in the path of the predicted lava flow from Kulahaleha.

'Ah yes, the slave-driver awaits. Are you sure about him? His feelings for his wife, I mean?'

Naomi scowled at him. Really, the man was too much. 'Yes I am,' she said flatly. 'Besides . . .' She glanced out of the big panoramic windows, her eyes blind to the spectacular sights. 'I saw a picture of Veronica once.' It had been in a prestigious magazine, for she'd been the daughter of a prominent landowner, and something of a high society darling.

Danny's eyes softened at the look of pain on her face.

'Yes?' he said softly. 'And?'

'And she was beautiful,' Naomi said flatly. 'Really beautiful.'

And with that she turned and left.

Danny watched her stiff-backed figure until it was out of sight, then sighed. 'What a pity,' he murmured sadly.

And ordered another okolehao.

'I was right,' Riordan said the moment Naomi walked through the door of the lab. The room was small, functional and crammed with equipment, but hardly underground, and was nothing approaching the dungeon of Danny's imagination.

Sat at his bench, monitors on, and the buzz of some programme running in the background, Riordan sat amid a pile of graph paper. 'Take a look. I tell you, Naomi, that mountain is getting ready to make us sit up and take notice.'

His excitement infectious, Naomi walked swiftly to where he was sitting and glanced over his shoulder, her eyes scanning the readings.

She didn't notice him tense as she laid one steadying hand on his shoulder, and missed the way his nostrils quivered just slightly at the scent of her shampoo as she leaned close to him, their faces only inches apart.

'You're right. The ground is on the move. What are the

latest seismograph readings?' she asked, but was already moving towards the big drum of smoked graph paper, looking them up for herself.

'Still no change,' Riordan said, watching her as she bent over the light box, the fluorescent tubes inside lighting her face with a yellow glow. It seemed to make her short hair shine with an almost divine radiance, he noticed.

She looked across at him, her eyes creased in puzzlement. 'I don't understand. What's going on?'

It was a good question.

'Come on, let's see what the GPS system has for us,' he said gruffly, and turned away.

Without a word, Naomi joined him, notebook to hand, his ever-faithful right-hand man.

It was nearly ten at night when they drove back to the Hilo Village Apartments, a three-storey accommodation block just off Waianuenue Avenue, near the Wailuku river. It had been assigned to them by the penny-pinching faculty and was beloved of tourists on a budget, and would be their home for the next two years.

It had a small pool in a central courtyard, a cheap and cheerful bar and café, and was, compared to some places where Naomi had lived over the years, a veritable paradise.

She could still remember life in a tent halfway up a volcano in southern America, so as she climbed stiffly out of the Jeep, the thought of soaking in her own bath, in an albeit cramped bathroom, sounded like bliss to her.

As they walked into the tiny foyer, music from the bar-cum-café wafting through the open archway, a man stepped up and looked across at them, smiling widely.

It was a particularly nasty smile.

In his mid-thirties, he was dressed in an Aloha shirt and plain white slacks. He had a tall drink in his hand, and was swirling the ice cubes inside it savagely.

'Well, well, well, if it isn't the oh-so-respected Dr Riordan Vane. And his sidekick, of course.'

As Naomi spun around in shock, the hatred in the voice making her pulse sky-rocket, she was aware that beside her Riordan had stiffened, like a dog scenting a rat.

When he turned to look at the man, however, his face was perfectly blank.

'Hello, Rudy,' he said flatly.

Chapter Three

Charis Scott smiled warmly at her secretary as she walked into the small outer office.

'*Aloha*,' Lehai greeted her cheerfully. She was a young girl, not long from college, and was extremely proud of her gold embossed desk sign, which proclaimed for all the world to see that Lehai Kaleohano was 'Secretary to Princess Mina'. Charis's long-time secretary had left last year to start a family, but Lehai was well on her way to filling her predecessor's shoes.

'The mayor called about Saturday night,' she said, as she handed Charis the folder of mail, neatly categorized into 'must answer', 'think about' and 'bin'. 'Will it be all right for him to bring a third guest? Some visiting baseball star from the mainland.'

Charis grimaced but smiled. 'Sure – the more the merrier.' She walked on through to her own office, where Lehai had already put on a carafe of coffee, and casually threw her purse on to the sofa. Then she went straight to the window, and opened it wide.

Charis Mina Scott (or Princess Mina to many of the old-family residents on the island) was a perfect advertisement for the beauty range which bore her name.

As she leaned out of the window, her ebony tresses waved and curled down her back to a tiny waist. She had to stand on tiptoe to lean out as, at only five-foot three inches, she was a constant slave to much-needed high-heeled shoes. Today she was wearing a plain white dress, square cut at the neck, and sleeveless. Her only jewellery was a gold choker made out of interlacing leaves, and a small gold watch.

A blossom of wild ginger was tucked into her hair behind one ear, for she was in the habit, when leaving home, of plucking some flower or other from the gardens on the way out, and putting it into her hair.

Her home, a large plantation-style residence which actually bore the name of 'palace', was already two centuries old, and lay just a mile or so down the road, and the thought of it, beloved but burdensome, made her sigh wearily.

She glanced around as the door opened, and Lehai walked in, going to the coffee machine. Charis took a seat behind her desk, a large, modern white-wood edifice which she kept practically bare, and smiled her thanks as Lehai put a steaming cup of fresh Kona coffee down in front of her.

'No word from the big man yet,' Lehai said cheerfully, 'but I checked that his plane landed safely yesterday. He's booked into the Hawaii Naniloa on Banyan Drive. Do you want me to send him a complimentary something-or-other?'

Charis sighed, propping off her white high-heeled shoes and contemplating her toes thoughtfully. 'No, I don't think so. I don't think he's the type for it.'

Lehai raised one dark eyebrow. 'No?'

Charis grinned. If there was one weakness her new secretary had, she'd discovered, it was the ability to gossip. And make Charis gossip right along with her.

'No. He's the self-made type. Hard as nails, from all I've read about the man,' Charis mused, feeling a familiar thrill.

When she'd first had the letter from Marsh Pharmaceuticals, expressing interest in buying out the Princess Mina range, the first thing she'd done had been to run a background check on the company. And one thing that had been immediately obvious was that Jago Marsh *was* the company.

She'd been fascinated as she'd read his dossier, perhaps because she'd been reading about a creature that she'd never encountered before. She was well aware that her own upbringing had been sheltered in the extreme. Even after she'd spread her wings and launched her own company, meeting with modest success and learning more about the world and how it worked, reading about Jago Marsh had told her that she was still a babe in the woods by comparison.

'He sounds intriguing,' Lehai said, not missing the warming colour seeping into her boss's cheeks. 'He's due in an hour. Did you want to talk to the troops?' she asked. 'You know, give them a pep talk?'

Charis smiled. 'No reason to. We'll be doing the usual tour. I don't want anything special laid on.' She frowned thoughtfully. 'To tell you the truth, I'm still not sure what he's doing here.'

Lehai perched one half of her bottom on Charis's desk, one eyebrow arched. Her relaxed attitude was a far cry from how she'd been when she'd first started work here. She'd been terrified of offending her boss, and was even now ever-mindful of her mother's warnings that Charis, in spite of her Americanized name, came from one of the oldest of royal lines.

Lehai had never met a real princess before, and had been

dumbfounded by Charis's beauty. Later, of course, as Charis had joked with her, taught her the ropes, and generally acted herself around the new girl, Lehai had come to like her for the person she was, not the title she carried. Now, she thought nothing of perching her pert bottom on Charis's desk and picking her brains. The one thing, though, that Lehai wasn't able to winkle from her was the state of her love-life.

On that subject, Charis was close-lipped. Now, the warm glow which suffused her cheeks made Lehai wonder.

'Have you ever met this Mr Marsh?' she asked craftily, and felt a shaft of disappointment lance through her as Charis shook her head.

'No, I never have. But from what I've read, I don't see why a company like Marsh Pharmaceuticals should be interested in buying us up. It just doesn't seem likely somehow.'

Lehai instantly bridled. 'Why not? We're the biggest-selling beauty range in the islands. All the chains want us.' And she should know – she'd been setting up meetings for her boss with all the big drug-stores for the past month or so.

Charis smiled. 'I appreciate your loyalty, Lehai, honest I do. And to you and me Princess Mina might well be the be-all and end-all. But to a giant like Marsh Pharmaceuticals – believe me, we're small fry. If I didn't know for a fact that they'd been testing the waters for some time now about branching out into cosmetics, I'd wonder if someone wasn't playing a practical joke on me.'

Lehai shook her head. 'You're too modest for your own good, Miss Scott.'

'Call me Charis,' Charis said automatically.

'I can't,' Lehai said, just as automatically. 'My mother would kill me.'

Charis grinned. 'Well, I suppose we'd better get the correspondence out of the way.' In fact, she was getting a bad case of butterflies in her stomach, and definitely needed something to take her mind off the upcoming meeting.

As she dictated and dealt competently with the matters in hand, another part of her pondered on why she was feeling so nervous. It was not as if Marsh's was the only offer she'd had. She could sell tomorrow to any one of the island's bigger chains, who'd be only too glad to own the Princess Mina range. Was it only because Marsh's was such a big, important company? Was she so shallow that the thought of attracting such a big fish had gone to her head? She didn't like to think her ego was that big.

Or was it the thought of meeting Jago Marsh himself that was so nerve-wracking? Somehow, she rather thought that it was.

As Lehai's pen flew over her notebook, and the clock ticked relentlessly on towards the hour of their meeting, Charis pondered on this new phenomenon. How could a man, one who she'd never even seen, talked to or imagined before, put these butterflies in her tummy, and this heat in her blood?

If she was strictly honest, she knew that she was intrigued, genuinely intrigued, for the first time in her life. Usually it was the men who did all the running, and she just had to sit back and watch.

But perhaps she could be forgiven for that.

She was the great-granddaughter of Parker Ford III, a wealthy Texan oil magnate, who'd come to the islands at the turn of the century, and fallen in love with Princess Mina, the only daughter of Prince Darius Kamalii.

He'd married her, over both of their family's objections, and moved into the big plantation house Charis had always called home. They'd had a daughter, who'd married another wealthy

American called Scott. Their only child, Darius, had been Charis's father.

So growing up a sheltered princess of Hawaiian royalty, and a much sought-after heiress of old-time American oil money, had hardly equipped her to deal with a man such as Jago Marsh.

Even within the dry lines of her business investigator's report on him, Charis had sensed the raw power the man must have needed to rise from a London slum to become one of the richest men in the country.

Charis looked up to see Lehai gazing at her, a knowing smile beginning to tug at her lips. 'Daydreaming?' she asked softly. 'About anyone in particular?' she teased.

Charis flushed. 'Nobody loves a smart arse,' Charis said, using one of her rare slang words. She'd been taught elocution by Miss Ferrars, who would no doubt have turned white as a sheet if she'd heard her royal pupil use such language.

But since her parents had been killed in a plane crash, their small plane falling into the Pacific Ocean between the islands of Oahu and Hawaii during a brief tropical storm, Charis had had no other option but to come out of her cocoon.

The family money was invested long-term, but her home was in need of constant maintenance. Her grandfather had suffered a stroke, and with the house feeling unbearably empty, she'd needed to get out, to make her own way in the world, and, incidentally, to earn some money for herself.

At twenty-two, she'd told herself she must be capable of that, surely. But then she'd sat down and taken a long hard look at herself. What, after all, did she know? What was she good for? Her education was suited to that of a woman who expected to marry young, and marry rich. She could arrange a dinner party, even cook some cordon bleu dishes. She could dress exquisitely, and command an A-list guest list, simply by putting her name on an invitation. But that didn't amount to hard cash at the turn of the last millennium.

It had been, ironically enough, an enamoured but slightly drunk fellow party guest, who'd first put her on to the solution. With her looks, he'd drunkenly gushed at her, she could be a Polynesian Helen of Troy. And would she like to launch his new yacht? He'd bought it for the regatta season stateside.

She had declined to christen his yacht, but had taken his other words into consideration. What did she know? Fashion, beauty products, jewellery, partying, charity work and poise. She knew, in fact, all about what a woman needed to keep herself beautiful.

It was hardly a business degree, work experience or capital. But it had been enough.

A talk to her favourite bank manager had sorted out the capital. And when word got around that she was looking to start up a business, things began to move.

And in sometimes unorthodox ways.

An old, old woman, who was rarely seen away from her shack in the woods, suddenly sent her an envoy in the form of a granddaughter. And what this lady didn't know about herbal beauty potions wasn't worth knowing. An old schoolfriend put her in touch with her brother, who'd just finished Harvard Business School, and he came up with a blinding publicity plan for the all-herbal range. Shops were only too glad to have 'royal' connections, and fell over themselves to buy.

Of course, it had started out small. She'd rented these offices and workhouses, which were almost on the edge of the forest and consequently going very cheap, and had set about planting much of the stock they now used today.

The old hermit woman's recipes soon became famous amongst the island's female population, as they really did seem to reduce wrinkles, chase away spots, cleanse and tone. Lipsticks suited to the vibrant island colours became ultra popular with the teenage market, whilst breathtakingly expensive herbal baths, soaps and shampoos became the 'must have' item amongst the super rich, super sophisticated element. And now the workshops were full, the gardens constantly expanding to take more herbs, flowers and native 'weeds', as Lehai would insist on calling them.

And Charis, for the first time in her life, it seemed to her, was now part of the real world. She had people depending on her for more than just her appearance at a charity dinner. She had meetings with accountants and advertising firms, not just with manicurists and hairdressers. She was seen as a 'player' by the business world now, not just by the paparazzi.

She wished she didn't have to sell.

The buzzer on the desk warned Lehai that they had a visitor, and with a squeak she shot out the door, something in Charis's own nervousness at last transferring itself to her. Charis too shot to her feet, and walked anxiously over to the mirror on the opposite wall.

Outside she could hear the call of an elepaio, the fly catcher who'd set up a nest not far from her office, and wondered if she should shut the window. Didn't a lot of visitors to the island prefer air conditioning? She herself liked the trade winds and sultry air, but perhaps she ought to close it.

She cast her reflection a quick look. With her simple white dress and raven-black hair, she knew she looked stunning. She was wearing, of course, Princess Mina make-up, which emphasized her big dark eyes and naturally full mouth.

Her shoes! She was standing there in her bare feet. She

rushed to her desk, slipped them on, turned to the window to close it, heard the door open behind her, and shot back around.

'Mr Marsh, your royal highness,' Lehai said, earning a quick furious look from Charis. Lehai knew she hated being called by her title, referring to it as outdated and irrelevant in this brave new millennium. But her secretary would insist on using it to impress visitors.

Looming above her secretary, Charis looked for the first time at Jago Marsh.

And felt her heart leap.

It was such a physical sensation that she felt her hand go to her throat, as if to keep it physically in place, and had to force a smile on to her face.

Jago walked further into the room, surprised by its clean lines and lack of clutter. He'd expected display cabinets full of geegaws and posters of models on the walls in full Princess Mina war paint.

Instead the room was painted in white and pale green, with rush matting on the floors and comfortable-looking chairs. Even the big blond-wood desk was free of papers.

Then he allowed his eyes to fall to the woman standing beside the desk, and their eyes met.

Nothing in Jago's face moved.

Charis, for her part, simply stared at him.

She hadn't expected him to be blond. Somehow, from the description of his life, she'd imagined a dark-haired man, thick-set and pugnacious.

Jago moved forward, lean and tall, and held out a hand. It didn't have so much as a signet ring to decorate it.

Charis forced herself forward, making her smile stretch even wider, although it already felt stiff and artificial on her face.

'Mr Marsh. I'm so glad you could come. I trust the flight went well?'

She sounded like an official tour guide welcoming his latest coachload of trippers. Why didn't she just put a lei of plumeria flowers around his neck whilst she was at it? So much for her famous poise.

Jago smiled briefly. 'Miss Scott?' he said, almost as if he doubted her identity.

As indeed he did.

He'd come expecting to find the hard-bitten, stuck-up predatory witch that had used and dumped his brother.

He hadn't expected to find . . . *her*.

She was tiny. Already he felt gauche and clumsy beside her. And why wasn't she in the ubiquitous power suit? Every female executive he'd dealt with to date seemed to wear the same uniform of dark navy designer suit and 'statement' accessories.

This woman looked dressed for a day at the beach. Or for lunch in some swanky hotel. At least he was wise enough in the way of haute couture to know that a deceptively simple dress such as hers meant bespoke tailoring and a hideously expensive price label.

'Yes. Please, won't you sit down? Lehai, something cold to drink, I think. Does the humidity bother you? I was just about to close the window.'

Charis grimaced inwardly as she heard herself babbling.

Jago glanced at the open window, surprised to see gardens beyond the glass, frothing with colour and perfume. And yes, now that he thought about it, he could definitely hear some birds singing.

Hardly the corporate car park he was used to seeing from his own warehouse office.

'No, I don't mind the heat,' he said truthfully. He'd found, on arriving at the islands, that the humidity hadn't bothered him at all. He was dressed in a lightweight cream suit and a charcoal-grey shirt and silvery tie.

The colour, Charis thought, brought out the silver in those magnificent eyes of his. She wondered who dressed him, and imagined his lover, a sophisticated Parisienne, perhaps, or one of those famous English-rose types, checking out his wardrobe for him and steering him right.

For there weren't many men who knew how to dress.

The thought of the woman in his life depressed her, and as she sank behind the desk, glad to place some neutral territory between them, she told herself firmly to pull herself together. She was behaving like an idiot.

Lehai came back with a jug of fruit juices swimming with ice and fruit, and placed it and two glasses on to the desk. Charis was glad when she poured out the drinks, for she could feel her own hands trembling. Luckily they were hidden beneath the desk.

Jago put down his briefcase by his side and leaned back in the chair. It was a swivel office chair, in black leather, and surprisingly comfortable.

The bright sunlight illuminated his face, and the white scar, mercilessly.

Charis found herself looking at the jagged line and wondering how he'd come by it. It looked as if it had caused him pain. A car crash, perhaps? Losing her own parents to a fatal accident made her sensitive to such things.

'It was a broken beer bottle,' Jago said calmly, his grey eyes managing to look both bored and amused somehow.

Charis bit her lip. 'I'm sorry, I wasn't aware that I was staring. I was just thinking that it must have hurt you.'

Lehai gave her a quick, puzzled look, and Charis felt like kicking herself. She wasn't normally this gauche. In fact, she'd considered socialising to be one of the things she did best. She'd been known to beat diplomats in the art of diplomacy, and even out-flatter semi-professional gigolos in her time. So why was she floundering about like someone standing on their own tongue?

Jago saw the mortified flush come and go on her face, and wondered what the hell was going on. If she was acting, she was doing it extremely well. But why bother?

'Please, won't you drink?' she offered, taking her own glass and swallowing nervously.

Jago took the glass, finding the tropical fruit taste pleasant and fresh, and looked up as a bird hopped on to the window ledge behind her. It was bright scarlet, and had a slender, hooked beak.

He blinked. 'We have a visitor,' he said, making Charis swivel her chair around in surprise, frightening it off, but not before she'd caught a glimpse of its plumage.

'It's a I'iwi,' she said, and, seeing the blank look on his face, added helpfully, 'A honey creeper. We've got quite a few different species of them on the island. They come here because of the herbs and flowers we grow in the gardens. Nearly half of the ingredients we use in the range are grown on site. They're then treated by the chemists and other experts in one annexe, and packaged in the main workshop. Would you like to see?'

Jago wondered if the pride and quiet satisfaction in her voice could possibly be put on, and again wondered why she should bother.

'Sure, why not?' he agreed. Now that he was here, he might as well play along.

As she rose and moved around the desk, he caught the

scent from the flower in her hair. Now how twee was that? What woman wore flowers in hair in this day and age? Was she really trying to con him into thinking she was some simple island girl?

They walked out through the foyer, Lehai half-rising to her feet and then sinking back. Her eyes, as she watched the tall Englishman walk by, were wistful.

Outside, Jago blinked in the bright sunlight and reached into the top pocket of his suit for his sunglasses. Charis led him from the manicured lawn and traditional rose beds of the front of the office, through a side gate and out into the main gardens themselves – a frothing, foaming, perfumed mass of colour. He was immediately aware of the drone of bees, and the ever-present call of birds. In the distance, a snow-capped volcano provided an almost impossibly dramatic and lovely backdrop.

Several gardeners laboured amongst the rows of herbs, bushes, trees and flowers, all of them raising a hand in greeting as they passed.

'*Aloha*, Kimo.' Charis paused beside one white-haired man, who looked up with a face as creased and cracked as that of a nut. 'How's Kama today?'

'Getting better, thank you,' the old man said, and smiled, revealing darkened teeth.

Charis smiled and carried on.

Jago didn't ask who Kama was, or what was wrong with him or her. If, for some reason of her own, Charis Scott wanted to play the lady bountiful, she could do it without him providing an audience.

'This is the processing plant,' Charis said, walking up to a long, low, wood-built building, and laughed. 'Sounds grand, doesn't it, but really there's very little "processing" that goes on. As you know, all of our ranges are herbal and based on ancient recipes, with no animal-testing, and the absolute minimum of chemicals. But it is an interesting place. Come on inside – I'll have to ask you to wear some protective clothing, though.'

So saying, she stepped into a small ante-room, handed him a heavy white suit, and climbed proficiently into an all-in-one suit herself. She even pulled up the hood, piling her mass of dark hair inside with no sign of hesitation.

Jago did likewise, annoyed that he wasn't able to do so as easily as she did. And then he realized what this meant. Charis Scott was used to donning this suit, which covered everything from your shoes to the hairs of your head. Ergo, she came in here often. Ergo, she was a hands-on sort of employer.

And again he felt himself to be wrong-footed. He'd imagined that Princess Mina, also known as Charis Scott, would never so much as set one daintily shod foot on the factory floor – much less cover up all that curvaceous and cultivated beauty with a thick space-suit.

'Come on and I'll show you how to make eye shadow,' she said, and grinned.

She couldn't help it.

There was something so uncompromisingly hard and masculine about Jago Marsh, especially dressed in the thick protective suit with only his mirrored sunglasses and scarred face showing, that the thought of something as feminine as eye shadow made her want to giggle.

Luckily, she refrained.

Inside, Jago was given a quick but salutary lesson in the art of taking herbs and making them into cosmetics. Most of the workers were women, he was surprised to note, but some were men, and those he spoke to were obviously very knowledgeable and culled from the university's science departments.

Outside, it was quieter and cooler, and the freshness of the breeze made him breathe deeply in appreciation. Not that the working environment inside had been unpleasant: the workshop had been well lit, air-conditioned and incredibly clean. But it was a far cry from the ultra-sterilized, white, soulless factories which produced the backbone of Marsh Pharmaceuticals' products. He'd even, around the white encompassing hoods, noticed that several of the women workers had flowers in their hair, also.

For some reason, that simple little fact made him feel angry.

'Do you want to see the packaging department?' Charis asked, as she climbed out of the suit. It left her long wavy black hair mussed around her face and shoulders. He wanted, for one insane moment, to push it back behind her ears, to smooth it down with his hands, and run his fingers through it.

He looked hastily away. 'No, that won't be necessary. It's much smaller than I thought,' he said, meaning to sound unimpressed, and followed her back into the main offices.

'It's small but our outlay is impressive,' Charis said defensively. 'And, of course, our corner of the market is assured. Anyone who buys the Princess Mina range will be getting a guaranteed market percentage. Lehai, bring in the latest marketing figures, will you, please?' she asked, on her way past her secretary.

Lehai nodded, watching Jago go by with speculative eyes. At first she'd been ambivalent about the Englishman. He looked pale, compared to the men on the islands, with that kind of fairness only northern Europeans sported. And that scar. And those grey eyes – such a steel-like colour. But he had something. Oh yes, no doubt about that, Lehai thought, as she deposited the file on her boss's desk and shot the Englishman another glance.

Charis watched her secretary leave with a smile hovering over her mouth. Then she caught Jago's eye and the smile fled. There was something . . . hard . . . about this man, which went beyond mere business. She couldn't quite put her finger on it, but she felt as if he didn't like her. Which was absurd, of course. He didn't even know her.

'So, what do you think?' she asked guilelessly.

Jago smiled. Was that supposed to be chutzpah? If so, she didn't have the face for it. She had a face for kissing.

He drew in his breath harshly, wondering where the hell that thought had come from, and said coldly, 'I'll need to know more, of course. You have a package for me?'

Charis did, and withdrew the document from her desk. It was designed, of course, to present the Princess Mina range in the best possible light, but it was honest. He'd find no chicanery in it, of that she was sure.

Just as she was sure that he'd check.

'I'm having a party on Saturday. It's my grandfather's birthday. Would you like to come? Then, perhaps sometime next week, we can discuss this further?' she suggested, determined to keep it pleasant.

Jago smiled. 'I'd be delighted.'

Would it be on display? Surely it would. Her family had owned the statue for generations. He couldn't imagine it wouldn't be there for all the world to see.

'Do you know the islands at all? My home is not far from here, actually – only about two miles outside Hilo itself.'

Jago held up his hand. 'That's all right, I know where it is.

My brother was a regular guest there last year,' he added silk-ily.

And was satisfied to see her pale.

Charis blinked. His brother. Marsh. Not ... surely not *Keith* Marsh?

'I knew a Keith Marsh once,' Charis forced herself to say, her words coming out tight and hard. 'Your brother?'

Jago's eyes narrowed. Why was she looking so angry? 'Yes. My little brother Keith,' he confirmed.

Charis smiled tightly and got up. 'Well, well. It's a small world,' she said, her voice unmistakably dismissive now. 'Until Saturday then,' she said, showing him to the door.

Jago abruptly found himself outside. Never, he realized, unsure whether to laugh or growl, had he been kicked out of a place so fast.

But why was she so antagonistic? It was Keith who'd been treated badly. She was acting as if she were the injured party. Bloody woman. With her flower in her hair and those big brown eyes. He shook his head, like a cat angrily dislodging a fly, and stalked to his car.

Inside, Charis sank into her chair. Keith Marsh's brother. Of all the rotten luck!

Chapter Four

Jago drove south out of Hilo, noting the low-storeyed build-ings, and wondering why the capital city had none of the high-rise glamour of Oahu's Honolulu, or Waikiki waterfront. On Kanoelehua Avenue he wound down the window of his rented car, and felt the evening breeze on his face. It smelt of the ocean and some perfumed flower which seemed rife on this part of the island.

He kept his eyes open for the turn-off on to Volcano Road, remembering from Keith's description that Charis lived off the same road that led to the Volcanoes National Park, and the impressive crater of Kilauea.

It didn't take him long before he saw two stone pillars, spanned by a length of wrought-iron gate. Above, the words 'Kokio Aloalo Palace' were spelt out in gilt-faced iron.

A man on the gate checked his invitation, which had been sent to him by courier, and waved him through, telling him the best place to park as he did so. As he wound through exotic-looking trees and shrubs, he got a glimpse of lights interspersed through the leaves, and then suddenly he was driving out into the open and the big sprawling house, or rather palace, was laid out in front of him. Incongruously, it reminded him of something from out of *Gone With the Wind*, with porticoes, white-painted stone work and big French windows. A wide wooden veranda circled the front of the house, and the odd turret or two gave it a touchingly naïve Gothic look. He supposed, over the years, the owners had all tried to stamp their own personality on it, producing this out-of-kilter but beautiful building.

He parked the car and walked up the wide wooden front steps, the stained-glass pair of double doors in front of him opening, as if by magic, to admit him. But then a dark-faced butler appeared and led him into a wide hall, already milling with people. In the rooms leading off the main hall he could see tables groaning with food, and waiters and waitresses circling with trays of drinks, a lot of them decorated with flowers and little cocktail umbrellas.

'Mr Marsh, so glad you could make it.'

As he heard a familiar voice, he pivoted on his heel to face her, and felt his breath falter, becoming trapped somewhere in the region of his heart.

She was dressed in figure-hugging silk the colour of flame, which seemed to burn the very air around her as she moved. She had on gold eye shadow and an almost amber shade of lipstick, which continued the fiery theme, making her look like fire personified. The silk clung to her breasts, tiny waist and thighs like an impetuous lover, and, yes, there was a huge orange flower in her hair, which tonight was caught up in an intricate chignon of whorls and loops.

'You had no trouble finding us, it seems,' she said, smiling politely.

He was dressed in a black tuxedo, which did very good things for his wheat-coloured, neatly cut hair and grey eyes. He looked dark and predatory, standing in her hallway, look-ing at her out of that lean, mean face of his, and she smiled again, just to show him that she was not afraid of him. The brother of a worm like Keith Marsh, she firmly reminded herself, could hardly be someone to worry about. Or think about. Not that she'd been able to stop thinking about him, ever since that first meeting at her office. The man had a nasty habit of popping into her head at the most annoying of times.

'Please, let me get you a drink. We have everything from cocktails served in half coconut shells, to piña coladas, blue Hawaiians and okolehao. Then there's champagne, of course, or . . .'

'Do you have beer?' Jago asked, feeling riled into playing the oaf.

Charis didn't bat an eye. 'Oh yes, all kinds. Would you prefer English or domestic?'

Jago smiled wryly. Score one for the princess. 'Anything will do. It's a warm night,' he said tightly.

'It always is in Hawaii,' she said, and then blinked. Had that sounded provocative? She hadn't meant it to. She turned abruptly and led him into the throng inside the next room, where a band was playing traditional music. The man on the Hawaiian guitar was especially good, and was justly famous throughout the islands.

If Jago had been au fait with island society, he would have recognized the cream of the crop at the palace that night, but as it was he merely smiled and nodded randomly, trying to keep his eyes from Charis's swaying silk-clad bottom as she led the way to a bar.

Open French windows led on to a balustraded balcony, and once again, on the breeze, he caught the scent of exotic perfume. In the next room, couples were swaying to the music, which filtered throughout the whole house. He saw an old man in a wheelchair, talking animatedly to someone who'd just given him a gift-wrapped offering. Obviously the grand-father. He had the round, friendly face of many a native islander, and he seemed to be enjoying himself.

'It's cold. We Americans always serve it ice-cold, I hope that's not a problem,' Charis said, handing him a glass dripping with condensation. Jago took a long swallow and smiled briefly.

'Thanks.' His eyes, Charis noted, were going around the room with an eagle's keenness, resting mostly on the display cabinets. Most of Charis's family had been collectors in the past, some of porcelain, some of coins, some of ethnic statuary. The most famous of all their possessions was, of course, the *Heart of Fire*, the statue of Pele carved out of magma rock, as legend would have it, by a mortal lover of the goddess, in times long since past.

'If you'll excuse me,' Charis said, spotting an old friend coming through the door, 'I have other guests to see.' Just in case he mistakenly thought she was going to spend all her time dancing to his tune.

Jago nodded, not looking at all put out at losing her company. 'Of course,' he said smoothly, and took another sip of beer.

Simmering, and mentally calling him all the limited number of rude words that she knew, she left him to attend her duties.

Jago wandered to the buffet tables, looking in bemusement at the array of food, and wondering when he'd be able to get his first look at the statue. It was, after all, the main reason he'd come to Hawaii.

'A bit overwhelming, isn't it?' A dry voice spoke just behind him, and he turned to look at a man a few inches shorter than himself. He had the weather-beaten tanned face of an outdoors man, and very bright blue eyes. He was dressed in what looked like a years-old jacket, which had nevertheless been made by a very experienced tailor.

'Riordan Vane,' the man said, holding out his hand. 'I'm

relatively new to the islands myself but I'm beginning to get the lay of the land. That,' he added, pointing to what looked like a whole roasted pig, holding pride of place in the centre of the table, 'is Kaluna pig. It's roasted on a spit outdoors all day. Lomi-lomi salmon.' He pointed to another dish. 'Then you get your traditional lau lau, made from the root of the taro plant with fresh pork and butterfish, and cooked in an underground oven called an imu. You should try some – it's good.'

Jago grinned, instantly liking the fellow Englishman, and sensing in him no hidden agenda. Used to being courted, baited or sounded out by businessmen, Jago would have bet his last pound that this man didn't even know who he was.

'I'll take your word for it,' he said, holding out his own hand, liking the way the other man squeezed it hard, but not too hard. A man, Jago instantly realized, who had nothing to prove. 'I'm Jago Marsh.'

Riordan nodded, then reached for a plate and helped himself to the Tahitian dish of poisson cru – which comprised raw fish, sliced onions and vegetables in coconut milk. He glanced around the room at the women dripping jewels and the men dripping bored charm, a somewhat bemused, bordering on cynical, smile flitting across his face. 'Know any of this lot?' Riordan asked quietly.

'Not a one,' Jago admitted cheerfully. 'I'm here on business with our royal hostess. Know her?' he asked sharply. But Riordan was already, disappointingly, shaking his head. 'Never met her before, sorry. I'm just on the list as the token academic.' And seeing Jago's raised eyebrow, added casually, 'I'm a volcanologist, here for two years studying the little guy up yonder.' He pointed out of the window to where the smaller peak of Kulahaleha was visible under the bright, full moon.

'Sounds far more interesting than buying out a cosmetics

chain,' Jago said, with no real envy. Sensing this, Riordan grinned at him.

'I think it is,' he said simply. And the two men, vastly different but brothers under the skin in that room full of exotic women, exotic perfume and exotic food, grinned at each other.

'Is it my imagination or is that woman trying to get your attention?' Jago said, half pointing with his drink towards a pretty blonde dressed in white. Riordan turned, saw Naomi, and his face closed down.

Jago wondered why.

'Yes, she is. That's my research assistant, Dr Bridges. Excuse me, will you?' he said, moving off into the crowd, weaving in and out with the easy lope of a man used to walking long distances.

So it's like that, is it, Jago thought, with a smile of pity for the other man. How women and their claws would persist in making their presence felt.

Riordan felt himself tensing up, the closer he got to Naomi, and he wondered why. He'd been conscious of some kind of resistance or unease in himself ever since he'd first knocked on her door tonight.

The invitation to come to Charis Scott's party had been a bolt out of the blue, until one of the administrators at the observatory had told him that it was a habit of hers to invite visiting academics to her soirees. He'd advised Riordan to accept, as there were always interesting and influential people to be found at a Charis Scott 'do', and to wear something upmarket and have a good time. The invitation had been for two, and Riordan had asked Naomi to come as a matter of course. Never one for socializing, he nevertheless knew enough to know that he would be expected to come with a presentable female guest, and he knew no-one else on the island to ask.

But the moment Naomi had opened the door to her little cramped flat, looking stunning in a long, simple white dress, pearl drop earrings and a splash of scent which tickled his nose deliciously, he felt he'd made a mistake.

Now he smiled briefly and lifted an eyebrow in query. 'You all right?'

'Yes, fine, thanks,' Naomi said, in some surprise. 'Isn't that Harris McVie over there?' she added, her words instantly chasing away any personal dilemmas as business took over. For Harris McVie held some very important purse-strings, and Riordan had been trying to get a grant from his university's financial board for the past ten years. So far without success, but recently he'd been getting some very promising-sounding letters from the American university which employed McVie. If he could only button-hole the man himself, and explain his needs, and the importance of his research, he could get on with implementing his dream.

'Where? I can't see who you're pointing to,' Riordan said, craning his neck as he tried to pick out the man Naomi was describing from the crowd. Then his vision was abruptly filled by the view of a black-and-white-clad figure of Randolph Voight Carter III.

'You two look very snug and cosy,' he sneered, and Naomi, who had unthinkingly put her hand on Riordan's arm, hastily removed it. She felt a flush of colour stain her cheeks and wondered why she should feel so guilty.

Beside her, Riordan's blue eyes focused rapidly on the man in front of them, a chill seeming to radiate from his very skin. 'Rudy, gatecrashing again?' he asked flatly.

Rudy laughed. 'Not so, old chap, not so.' He was, Naomi guessed, in his late thirties, early forties, about two inches shorter than herself and Riordan, and had dark brown hair and dark hazel eyes. He had the kind of face that was ugly, but in an almost attractive sort of way. He wasn't, she supposed, the kind of man that most women would ignore.

When she'd first seen him, back at their apartment block a few days ago, Riordan hadn't introduced them but had carried on to the stairs, totally ignoring the man. With no other choice but to follow suit, Naomi too had gone to her room, and the next day hadn't been able to work up the courage to ask Riordan who he was. Though he had obviously been no friend.

And now, again, she could feel the mutual animosity between the two men almost as a physical force. She looked around anxiously, but nobody else at the party seemed to be aware of the trouble that was obviously brewing. She bit her lip nervously and looked briefly at Riordan. His profile was hard and cold. She'd never, she realized in dismay, seen him look angry before, and guessed that this was what she was seeing now. She didn't particularly like it. Her first instinct was to leap to his defence and show her support, willing to back him up, even though she'd be acting blind. But she instinctively knew he wouldn't thank her for it, and a warning little voice in the back of her head counselled her to keep her peace.

'I'm always invited to all the best dos. You know that,' the offensive little man was drawling now. 'The good old Carter name gets us in everywhere, even here. Not that our lovely hostess herself would know the English aristocracy from Adam, of course. But she has well-informed friends that do,' he added with unbearable smugness.

Naomi gasped, for suddenly she made the connection. Carter was the maiden name of Riordan's late wife, Veronica. Looking back on that time when, in her dentist's waiting room, she'd picked an upmarket home and garden magazine, and had seen a picture of Veronica Vane, Naomi realized that

72

there was a definite family resemblance to this man. Except that, in Veronica, there was nothing of the ugliness, only breathtaking beauty. But the lush dark hair and compelling hazel eyes were the same.

'How nice for you,' Riordan said flatly. 'What are you doing in the islands, Rudy?'

Rudy Carter smiled savagely. 'Oh, you know. The usual. And of course it's the anniversary coming up soon. I never like to be in England when that time rolls around.'

Riordan went white. Naomi's eyes widened as she saw his hands clench into fists, and wondered, for one wild, heart-stopping moment, if he was going to hit him. Obviously Rudy wondered too, for she saw him take a quick step back. Then Riordan sighed. 'Get out of my sight, Rudy,' he said flatly, his voice incredibly weary.

Sensing that he was safe, Rudy Carter smiled again. It was the sort of smile which made even Naomi's toe-nails curl, and it wasn't even directed at her.

'Feeling guilty, are we?' Rudy said, his mock-sympathy as cloying as molasses. 'Don't worry. I ordered a wreath in your name to be put on her grave.' And with that he turned and moved away.

Wreath. Of course, Naomi thought in dismay. Veronica had died on the 15 June, which was next week It had been six years since the accident had happened. So the 'anniversary' was a sad one.

Riordan turned away, caught Naomi's eye, and inwardly cursed. 'I'm sorry about that. Rudy has a . . . thing . . . about his sister's death. I was driving,' he said flatly, his staccato statements clearly indicating that he was very upset indeed.

Naomi wished the floor would open and swallow her up. 'I know. I mean, I guessed as much. But it's not your fault. I mean, it was an accident, wasn't it.'

Riordan looked at her strangely, and Naomi experienced one of those moments when everything seemed to freeze. The people around them. Time. Her own blood. She felt a shiver of portent snake down her spine as she wondered what the look in his eyes could possibly mean. But then, just as quickly as it had come, it was gone. The sound of laughter and conversation flowed back, the scents of food and wine and flowers, the rainbow colours of gowns and jewels all around her.

And she was left with a gossamer feeling which she couldn't put into words.

Riordan heard the Hawaiian guitar pick up a slow, impossibly lovely melody, and before he knew what he was doing he was reaching for her hand. 'Come on, let's dance,' he said gruffly, leading the way to the veranda, which was wide and spacious, and mostly deserted.

Naomi, hardly able to believe it was happening, let herself be led, telling herself that it really was his hand holding hers, that he truly was leading her out into the tropical night, and that the sound of music wasn't a cruel illusion after all. Then he was pulling her into his arms, and it was all she could do to keep on breathing. Normally they were exactly the same height but tonight she was wearing high-heeled shoes, and as their faces came together, her cheek rested just a shade higher on his face, and she could smell the clean scent of his hair. She wanted, desperately, to turn her lips just that fraction of an inch required and kiss his temples.

Her eyes feathered closed as their bodies swayed together to the sound of the Hawaiian guitar. Somewhere in the vast grounds, a pueo, an Hawaiian owl, called to its mate. It was all so perfect, she was almost convinced she must be dreaming.

Riordan's hand, resting lightly in the nape of her back,

seemed to hesitate before he firmly pulled her closer against him. He wondered what he was getting himself into; wondered if he was making a mistake. He wondered even harder if he wasn't being unfair to Naomi. He wondered, even, if he was going out of his mind. But their bodies seemed to fit like two perfect halves and surely, surely, he was entitled to one dance, to one brief moment of happiness.

Naomi felt her nipples hardening against his chest, and hoped against hope that he couldn't feel it. Her knees felt deliciously weak but she kept on dancing. She wasn't about to waste one precious moment of this time. But even as she danced, she knew that more was happening than the movement of their bodies. Somehow, something basic, something fundamental between them, had shifted. Tonight, for the first time, she was sure he was seeing her as a woman, that he was aware of her as another human being. He certainly wasn't holding her as if she were some magnetometer or gas thermometer.

Whatever the trouble was between him and his brother-in-law, it had shaken something loose in him, and she was going to take advantage of it. She knew it, even as she wondered if she was being incredibly ruthless. But she was a woman in love. Moreover, she was a woman who'd never sensed even a moment of reciprocation in the object of her desire. Until now. Perhaps the ghost of the beautiful Veronica was loosening her hold at last. Or perhaps he was just angry, a little out of control, and that it would never last. Perhaps tomorrow, when they were back at work, cocooned in their familiar, cold, scientific environment, he would be able to forget that this moment had ever happened.

She held him a little tighter. But perhaps not.

As the moon shone down on their swaying figures, as the Hawaiian guitar wailed its poignant tune, and she felt her heart beating strongly against his, she knew that she was going to try, with everything in her, to make Riordan Vane love her in return.

What, after all, did she have to lose?

Inside the main reception room, Rudy Carter watched Charis Scott with a kind of detached respect. She was lovely, of course, with her curvaceous petite figure and raven locks. What's more, she had the lure of royalty which was especially piquant, and she had brains as well. He'd be a fool not to admire her. But he wasn't smitten. He wasn't hooked, like many of the men who watched her so avidly tonight. Like that tall blond fellow countryman with the rather unfortunate scar, for instance.

Rudy briefly wondered what his story was, for, unless he was mistaken, there was some self-loathing mixed up with his desire. It was there in the way he watched her, a sardonic smile on his lips, as if he was beating himself up over something.

A good study of human nature, Rudy could see that the lovely Charis was every bit as much aware of the blond as he was of her. No matter how much both of them were going out of their way to ignore each other.

Feeling uptight after his run-in with that bastard Riordan Vane, and needing to vent his spleen on some mischief, Rudy put down his drink and put on his best look. It was a mixture of boredom, friendliness and mischievous twinkle which sat so well on his ugly-interesting face. And always worked a charm on the ladies.

'Miss Scott, you certainly know how to throw a party,' he said, seamlessly insinuating himself between his hostess and the tall, grey-haired man she'd been talking to. With a discreet murmur he excused himself, and Charis found herself looking up at a perfect stranger. It wasn't a new experience for her. 'Glad you could come, Mr. . . ?'

'Carter. But call me Rudy – everyone does. Would you like
to show me your gardens?' he added, deliberately outrageous.
'I hear they're famous. And what's all this about your palace
being named after a bush? Surely not?'

Amused but not misled by the come-on line, Charis was
about to give him a gentle brush-off when she spotted Jago
Marsh, blatantly eavesdropping just a few inches away, and
smiled widely instead.

'It's perfectly true, I assure you, Rudy,' she said, tucking her
arm flirtatiously into his and letting herself be led out of the
nearest set of French windows. She would show that rude
blond English upstart how a lady should be treated at her
own party. 'Legend has it that the very first native hibiscus
bush, the kokio aloalo, grew on this very site. That's why there
was an ancient heiau, an open-air temple, built right here,
way before recorded history began. Later, the legend got
corrupted, when one of my ancestors built a palace on this
spot and called it after the flower. Now legend has it that
there must always be a royal residence here, or the kokio
aloalo would die out, and never be seen again on the island.'

She didn't turn her head, and had no idea that Jago was
right behind her, listening with a grim smile to everything she
said. She certainly was full of herself, wasn't she? Jago
thought, as he stepped out on to the terrace, the heat and chatter of the party gradually filtering out to a mere whisper
behind him as they walked deeper into the gardens. Her
family this, her family that. Now they were responsible for the
very welfare of the island's ecology system. No wonder she
thought a mere working-class boy like Keith Marsh was too far
beneath her notice to be treated with even common courtesy.

But Jago didn't think the man she was with now was all that

impressed. He'd recognized the upper-crust accent from his days with his own erstwhile fiancée, and knew out of his own bitter experience that that particular type of snob was never impressed with anyone or anything except another of its own kind. What's more, Jago knew trouble when he saw it, and the ugly little twerp who had hooked on to her was definitely a fine example. So why was he feeling compelled to follow her about like some kind of bodyguard, ready to leap in and rescue her?

He found himself grinning savagely in the dark. Funny, he'd never thought of himself as the chivalrous kind before.

Ahead, Charis was leading the way to a rose arbour, feeling restless but also just a little amused by her new 'admirer'.

'So, is this a fine example of the species?' Rudy was saying, reaching out to a large, somewhat prickly-looking bush with thick succulent leaves and a big flower head, which looked dark brown in the night but he guessed would be bright scarlet in the daylight.

Charis laughed. 'Good guess, but no. That's an ohia lehua.'

'You don't say. I'm more familiar with rhododendrons myself.'

Charis laughed. She couldn't help it. The man was such a phoney. But she had a soft spot for buffoons.

In the darkness, though, her laughter sounded light and sultry, and in the moonlight her flame-coloured dress made her stand out like a beacon. They were sitting on a bench now, surrounded by the ghostly shapes of white roses.

'So when do I get to see this famous statue of yours?' Rudy said casually, making Jago Marsh almost stumble in surprise. He stood stock-still, peering through the gloom, wondering if perhaps he'd misread the man altogether. Could he be another collector?

Charis was wondering the same thing, and her tone was

markedly cooler as she replied, 'the *Heart of Fire* is in a locked case in the library. No doubt my grandfather has shown it to everyone who's expressed an interest. We're very proud of it in the family. It's been in our care for as long as anyone can remember. You know the legend about it, of course?'

Rudy shrugged. 'Can't say as I do. You really are very lovely, aren't you?' he said casually, and slung an arm around her shoulder.

Charis had had enough. Fondness for buffoons or not. 'I think we'd better get back,' she said, then gave a muffled yelp as he caught her wrist as she was getting up, making her fall back on to the bench.

Instantly, Jago was there. 'Let go of her,' he said, his voice quiet, almost pleasant, as it issued out of the night, but carrying a definite warning nevertheless. Both Charis and Rudy shot up, taken totally by surprise, and peered into the night. Jago stepped closer, the moonlight illuminating his fair hair and narrow face.

Rudy sighed theatrically, but there was nothing theatrical about the way his warning system was telling him not to mess with this man. 'Fine, fine, no offence meant, I'm sure. Princess Mina.' He bowed elaborately in her direction and sauntered off.

Charis didn't even bother to watch him go, for all her attention was instantly riveted on only one man.

'Did you follow me out here?' she asked abruptly. She'd meant to sound cold and angry but somehow her voice came out husky and feeble.

'I did,' Jago confirmed uncompromisingly. 'I thought you might need rescuing,' he added drily.

Charis felt her skin flame. A proper Sir Galahad, wasn't he. Did he think she was ten years old?

'Perhaps I'm perfectly capable of looking after myself.

Perhaps I only wanted a kiss under the moonlight,' she said, again intending to sound chilly and sophisticated, and appalled to hear an almost wistful note in her voice instead. 'Or did that not occur to you?'

'Well, in that case,' Jago said, taking a step that brought them only a breath apart, 'perhaps I can oblige you.'

Charis's pupils dilated, and again she gave a muffled yelp, this time as Jago pulled her off the ground, literally, and up into his arms. Her feet kicked helplessly in the air for a moment, and she just had time to give a scandalized, outraged, excited sigh before he was kissing her.

His lips were hard and yet somehow soft. His arms around her were like a vice, and yet she felt utterly safe. His body heat flamed more brightly than the colour of her dress and she felt herself sliding down, down, down his body, her senses also a victim of gravity, as her blood seemed to thicken sluggishly in her veins. Something wonderful pounded in her head, and then, without warning, she was free.

And back on the ground, his mocking face clearly visible in the moonlight.

'Feel better now?' Jago asked sardonically. But his heart was beating as if some demented drummer was playing on it.

Charis blinked. She wanted to slap him but something in the depths of his steel-grey eyes warned her not to.

Instead, she said something in Hawaiian, turned and stumbled away.

Chapter Five

Positive that whatever it was she'd just spat out in Hawaiian wouldn't be complimentary, Jago smiled widely and followed her leisurely through the gardens, back towards the noise of the party. In the moonlight, he easily kept track of her flame-coloured figure, and smiled yet again, wolfishly, as he contemplated how close he'd just come to having his face slapped.

The thought was neither humiliating nor annoying. In fact, he rather relished it. It was a pity, in many ways, that her royal highness had had such good survival instincts, and *hadn't* tried to slap him. He'd rather have liked to have seen the look on her face if she *had* tried it.

Up ahead, fuming, upset, unsettled and tingling all over, Charis strode up the stone steps to the veranda and disappeared inside, her spine ramrod stiff, her hips swinging, everything about her crying 'look out'.

Jago laughed out loud. He couldn't remember a time when he'd felt so alive. So invigorated. All his life it had been work, work, work. He'd forgotten, until now, that there could be far more to life than that.

Now, at least, he could see why Keith had fallen so hard and so disastrously. But just let Charis Scott try the same thing on with *him*.

Then he wondered, his lupine grin fading just a little, whether she'd still have the nerve to try and take him on. Or was she too smart for that? Somehow he hoped not. She'd stirred his blood now, and he wanted to know whether the promise of fire she'd shown tonight went more than skin deep.

Something was stirring inside him that had never been roused before, and he was intrigued by it. A little wary too. Something told him that Charis Scott could be one dangerous lady to know.

But he'd be careful.

He was always careful.

Riordan Vane accepted a glass of champagne from a passing waitress, who flashed him a very warm smile, and handed it quickly over to Naomi, who in turn pretended not to notice that the girl had been giving him the eye. She took a sip, glad of the cold, refreshing buzz it gave her, and glanced around curiously.

After their first dance, they'd kept well away from the wide open spaces, and now they were stood by a huge picture depicting the Napali cliffs. On the opposite wall, and almost certainly by the same artist, was a view of Kuhio harbour. In the hall outside, there was a stark, incredibly beautiful painting of the Kau desert, and Naomi wondered if their hostess bought a lot of local art, for she was sure the painter had to be a native to the islands. Only somebody who'd grown up with such vibrant colours could paint with such bold confidence.

'Which one is she, anyway?' Naomi asked, and when Riordan glanced at her curiously, added quickly, 'Our hostess, I mean. I've never met a real live Princess before.'

Riordan looked around vaguely. 'I'm not sure. You don't happen to see anyone bowing or scraping, do you?'

Naomi laughed. 'No. I haven't spotted any crowns either.'

Even as she smiled brightly, Naomi wondered with a pang if he'd ever ask her to dance again. She saw him looking at her and grappled desperately for something to talk about. But she'd never been in a situation like this before – a social situation – with the memory of their dance together still burning like a firebrand into her memory. And all she could think of to talk about was work.

'We've had some more seismic activity on the west flank, middle elevation,' she said, although she knew he'd almost certainly seen the readings for himself.

'Yes. Wait. Is that him?' he asked, pointing out a tall, very American-looking individual, and Naomi nodded quickly.

'Yes, it is,' she said excitedly. 'Come on.' And she plunged into the throng, her lean length and five foot ten inches allowing her to steer an easy course through the mêlée. So intent was she on catching up with her quarry that she almost caught at Harris McVie's sleeve, and just stopped herself in time. But behind her, over the beat of tuetti drums and ukuleles, she heard Riordan say, 'It's Mr McVie, isn't it? Of the UBF?'

Harris McVie turned, his eye first catching Naomi and then going beyond her to Riordan. He was a man of indeterminate middle age, with silvering hair and a narrow, florid face. His eyes, a shrewd brown, were obvious windows for the computer in his head. Naomi could almost swear she could hear his memory banks whirring away somewhere, and coming up with an answer.

'Dr Vane, isn't it?' The computer chip in his head was obviously working well. 'Ah yes, I remember now: the dean of the university told me you're here on a two-year grant from Cornell's. How are things going?'

It was the opening Riordan had been hoping for, and beside him, Naomi relaxed. If anyone could sell his research ideas, Riordan could.

'Very well. In fact, Kulahaleha might be small, as volcanoe's go, but she's very interesting. We're getting some anomalous readings, which are intriguing us all.'

Harris McVie, used to academics of all walks of life, listened politely, but was soon genuinely fascinated by the life of an active volcano.

Dr Vane's application for a grant to lease time from a revolutionary new GPS (global positioning satellite), which had been launched recently, was one of four shortlisted, awaiting a final decision from the finance committee of which he was the chairman. No doubt the scuttlebutt had got back to all four applicants, since the academic world was no more capable of keeping a secret than any other. So Harris wasn't particularly surprised to find himself being button-holed by Riordan Vane. When he'd been in Massachusetts, he'd had his ear bent by one of the other shortlisted candidates, an ecology expert who needed funding to set up a butterfly conservation/farm project in the Rwandan heartland.

'In fact, it would have been invaluable if we'd been able to make use of the GPS system right now on Kulahaleha. But of course that simply isn't viable.'

There was real regret in his voice, but Harris was used to high levels of commitment from the people he dealt with, and he wasn't about to let himself be emotionally blackmailed.

'I imagine so,' he said smoothly, his voice so non-committal that neither Naomi nor Riordan could possibly miss it.

Over by the bandstand, Rudy Carter was sipping at a hefty

draught of the local punch, a potent mixture of papaya, coconut and rum.

He was still fuming about being interrupted outside in the rose arbour, wishing now that he'd taken on that scarred freak and shown him where to get off. Then he caught sight of Riordan in the crowd and instantly he felt his innards clench. It was the same whenever he thought of his sister's killer; this same feeling of frustrated hatred churned his stomach, making him feel physically ill.

Look at him, that simpering blonde floozy by his side, hanging on to his every word as if it were gospel. And the great man himself, talking some poor sod's head off. Him and his bloody volcanoes. How Veronica used to complain to him bitterly about her husband's work.

Rudy and Veronica had always been close, being the only children of parents who'd had time for neither of them. Their mother had felt obliged to provide the family with an heir, but if he and Veronica hadn't been twins, he was sure his mother would never have given birth again. She seemed to find motherhood almost abhorrent, but had at least had the decency to hire a good nanny.

Good old Nanny Benn. Life would have been intolerable without her. Their father they had rarely seen, as he divided his time between the city, the country estate and his latest mistress. No wonder he and Veronica had grown up so close. She would tease him about his ugliness, but let any of her friends call him that and she'd come to his defence like a tigress. At night, they'd sneak midnight feasts and talk about the future. Always Veronica was going to marry someone rich and handsome, and Rudy was going to make more money than Daddy.

Funny how things turned out.

Rudy now lived on a remittance, paid by their father on the condition that he darkened the family's doorstep as little as possible, and Veronica. . . .

Rudy felt his eyes begin to swim with tears, and he hastily swallowed them back, along with a big gulp of punch.

And Veronica was dead. Lying in her grave in the country churchyard where all the other Voight Carters were interred. At thirty-two. All the beauty, all that life, all that passion, gone. Because of him.

Rudy studied the man Veronica had married, surprised that he didn't drop dead on the spot. If wishes could kill, Riordan Vane would be buried next to his sister right this second. Instead of standing there, breathing air, enjoying wine, talking so animatedly.

Rudy tensed. Yes, he was looking keen, wasn't he? Not at all the usual cool, calm, scientific academic he was used to seeing. What was going on?

Slowly, cautiously, not wanting to be seen, Rudy began to manoeuvre his way around the room.

Jago Marsh finally spotted the old man's wheelchair in the music room. Like most of the other downstairs reception rooms, this too was full of people, music and food, and he waited patiently until the old man's companions, an obvious husband-and-wife couple of advanced years, moved away.

'*Aloha*, sir. You must be Charis's grandfather?' Jago said smoothly, watching as the old man's arthritic fingers moved the little knob on the arm of the wheelchair and the silent battery-operated machine swung in his direction.

Jago saw at once that one side of his face was lower than the other, as if some cruel trick of gravity was heavier on that side, and realized the man was the victim of a stroke. But the eyes were keen and bright, and when they ran over him, taking inventory of his scarred face, extremely expensive Philippe Patek watch, Savile Row tailored tux and pale skin, he felt sure that he'd just been catalogued by an expert. But whether the old man approved of what he saw or not, Jago couldn't tell.

He smiled, just briefly, to show that he didn't care, and could have sworn the old man's eyes twinkled just a little bit more.

'I'm Jago Marsh. Your daughter and I might have business to discuss,' he said smoothly.

'Oh yes. The man who owns the drugs and medical supply factory.'

Jago blinked, then smiled. Score one for the old geezer. Marsh Pharmaceuticals, he was sure, had never been so dismissively described before. What was it with this family? They all seemed determined, in one way or other, to extract their pound of Marsh flesh.

'That's right. The same *factory* that's put in an offer for your granddaughter's little herbal shop.'

The old man made a wheezing sound which, for a moment, alarmed Jago, until he realized that, far from having a coughing fit, the old scoundrel was laughing.

He was dressed in lightweight white slacks and shirt, which did nothing to disguise the thin desiccated body, but which suited his mane of white hair and darkly tanned skin perfectly.

'I just saw my granddaughter a while ago,' the old man mused, his voice only slightly slurred. 'She was coming in from the garden, and looked as if someone had just lit a fire-cracker underneath her.'

Jago couldn't help but grin.

'Guilty,' he said, unrepentantly. 'But, in my defence, she did ask for it.'

The old man cocked his head to one side, his eyes thoughtful. 'Did she now?' he said, his voice thoughtful. 'That doesn't sound like Charis.'

Jago's eyes instantly sharpened on the old man. 'No?' He was surprised to hear it. He'd have said this old-timer was both a very good judge of character and as sharp-eyed as an eagle, but perhaps age and illness had taken the edge off him.

Certainly, if he thought his granddaughter was still Little Miss Wonderful, the poor beggar was definitely misguided.

'So, what can I do for you, Mr Marsh?' Charis's grandfather asked crisply, and Jago smiled.

'What makes you think there's anything you can do for me?' he asked, rather enjoying this mental game of chess. Despite his blind spot as far as his family was concerned, he was sure this old chap would make a fine opponent.

The old man smiled, his mouth drooping on one side and giving him a slightly grotesque look. But it was impossible to feel sorry for him, and Jago had no intention of so insulting him.

'Well, when a young man at a party overflowing with beautiful women and choc-a-block with booze, chooses to seek out the company of an old man, I don't figure that he wants the pleasure of my company.'

Jago laughed. 'True. I was wondering if you would show me the *Heart of Fire*.'

The old man tilted his head back to get a better look at the tall blond man in front of him, his mind working rapidly.

Not your typical *haole*, that was for sure. Nor your typical businessman. And if this scarred *malahini* wanted to buy out his granddaughter's Princess Mina range, he'd eat his hat.

But there'd been something in his voice when he talked of the statue just now. Oh yes. There had definitely been something in his voice then.

'But of course, it would be my pleasure. It's kept in the library. Won't you follow me?'

Jago, who would have followed him to the ends of the earth to get his first look, face to face, with the famous statue of Pele, followed silently, his own mind working furiously.

Just how much money was it going to cost him to get his hands on it?

Rudy was now just where he wanted to be, standing behind a tall and, more importantly, very wide man, dressed in pale blue slacks and an incredibly bright floral shirt. Some people just had no idea how to dress. But although he couldn't see Riordan and his so-called research assistant, he could hear them plainly. And the blonde's voice, whenever she talked to Vane, positively oozed devotion.

How many times had Veronica complained to him about the hero-worshipping female students Riordan always seemed to attract? How many times had she cried drunkenly on his shoulder, when Riordan was away in the wilds of South America, or risking his neck on the erupting Mount Etna, or just working late – yet again – at the labs? She'd always been sure he'd been sleeping with every female in sight. Certainly with every research assistant or grad student he hired.

Of course, Rudy had tried to assure her he wasn't. The man would be mad to even look at another woman. She was Veronica Carter – sometime model, society hostess, darling of the English aristocracy, prime paparazzi fare. Her boring old fart of a husband should worship the very ground she walked on. All women looked like donkeys compared to her.

And Veronica would laugh, and they'd drink another drink, and dish the dirt on their friends, and feel better. Rudy was always able to make her feel better. Until the next time. Not that he minded his sister's emotional stranglehold on him. He understood that she needed not only to be loved, but to be adored. Not just admired, but worshipped. Why hadn't that lout of a husband of hers understood that?

Rudy had never understood why Veronica had chosen him in the first place. She'd had offers of marriage from an earl's son, and a supermarket heir. But no, she had to have Riordan. He was so sexy, she'd said to him once, giggling on the night before their wedding. So upright. So deliciously and wonderfully strong.

Yes, Rudy thought now, straining his ears to hear what Riordan was talking about so earnestly to the big red-faced American stranger. Perhaps that was it. Veronica had needed someone strong.

For Veronica had always been so weak. So unstable. So needy.

'That's why the GPS system is so vital,' Riordan was saying now, and Rudy almost snorted out loud. Volcano-speak. Was that all the man could do?

No wonder poor Veronica had been driven out of her mind. Five years married to a man who could only talk about volcanoes. It was no wonder she'd turned to Prozac. Booze. Clinics. Dramatics. Other men. And then all those suicide bids . . .

'I can understand why you're so keen.' The drawling American voice came right out of a TV western, Rudy thought disgustedly. Good ol' John Wayne rides again. 'But as you know, the committee doesn't meet until next month. But as soon as a decision has been made, I'll let you know straight away. That's a promise.'

Riordan nodded, knowing it would be useless to talk any more but feeling satisfied with what he'd accomplished. Everyone knew that Harris McVie was the guiding light on that committee, a man who knew both the financial and the academic world. It would be on his say-so whether or not the grant came their way, and he was sure he'd captured the man's interest. He'd especially tried to impress on him the need for an early warning system on volcanoes in densely inhabited areas. It could save lives. Many lives.

Rudy carefully turned away as the tall American moved off, and Riordan almost caught him eavesdropping.

'I think that went well,' Naomi said. 'You could see he was interested, especially in your theory about gas and particle clouds. And the idea of saving lives really gave him food for thought, you could see that.'

Rudy sighed elaborately. Yadah-yadah-yadah. Even the blonde bombshell was as boring as old sobersides himself.

'Yes, I think you're right. He seemed like a fair-minded sort of man. Well, we'll just have to keep our fingers crossed. If we *don't* get that funding for the year after next, we'll be back to square one.'

Riordan looked at her thoughtfully. He wanted to ask her to dance again, he realized, a little surprised by the sudden revelation. The thought of holding her close, of forgetting about work for once, of doing something outrageous, maybe even dangerous, was almost overwhelming.

And by dangerous he didn't mean dressing up in an asbestos suit and walking right up to the lava flow of an erupting volcano to take gas samples. Nor risking his life by getting caught in a pyroclastic throw. But risking his heart. Risking involvement again.

After his wife had died, he'd thought he'd never want to

look at another woman again. Had never even been able to imagine risking so much of himself, putting his welfare in the hands of another woman.

Not after what happened with Veronica.

But Naomi was so utterly different from anyone he'd ever met before. She understood him, and shared his passion for mountains that spit fire. She was mature, and really quite beautiful. He blinked. Why hadn't he noticed that before? Her hair and her eyes were lovely.

'Come on,' he said softly, holding out his hand. 'Let's dance.'

And as Naomi's face lit up, Rudy Carter nearly choked on his drink. Was that indulgence he'd heard in Riordan's voice just then? And since when did he dance? Veronica, a fine dancer, had always griped about never being able to get her husband out on to the dance floor, or even to a party.

Had she been right, after all? Had Riordan Vane been sleeping with his research assistant all this time?

As he watched them move into each other's arms, and he saw the short-cropped blonde head resting against Vane's shoulder, where the full brunette head of his sister should have rested, Rudy felt his hatred harden.

It seemed to shrink in on itself, like a collapsing star, leaving a black hole which consumed him. And with its birth came a new birth. A promise. This time he was going to do something. This time he wasn't going to get roaring drunk on the anniversary of his sister's murder. This time he was going to avenge her.

The only question was – how?

'And here she is.' The slurred voice was soft, almost hushed, with reverence, and Jago felt himself tense as the gnarled old hands lifted down the black, smooth rock.

He placed it carefully on the small occasional table, which stood beside the display cabinet for just that reason, and moved his hands away.

His eyes were fixed, however, not on the *Heart of Fire* statue, but on that of Jago Marsh.

The old man nodded. A collector. He'd been sure of it before but it was nice to get confirmation.

For his part, Jago stared at the statue as if mesmerized. Finally, he spoke. 'I've read a description of it which called the piece "unfinished". It described the head and shoulders and the lava flow perfectly. But words can never describe it. Why did you never let it be photographed?'

Charis's grandfather shrugged. 'Our forefathers didn't trust or understand photography. You have to remember, the *Heart of Fire* has been in our family since before written records were kept, let alone photography being invented. I dare say we thought it might try to take the soul of the goddess away from her, or from the stone. And since then, it's become a tradition, a superstition, if you prefer, that the *Heart of Fire* never be photographed. But you must have seen drawings of her.'

'Oh, I have,' Jago said, moving forward, unaware that the old man's eyes had suddenly moved beyond him, to the figure standing in the doorway.

Charis, whose mouth was open, ready to say something, snapped her lips together firmly at her first sight of his blond visitor. She'd come in search of her grandfather to make sure he'd taken his medication. Sometimes, in the excitement of entertaining, he could forget.

She hadn't been surprised when the butler had informed her that he'd seen him go into the library, but she hadn't expected to find him with Jago Marsh of all people.

Well, he could just damn well leave. Once again her mouth opened, about to tell the Englishman in no uncertain terms that he was no longer welcome in her house, when he did something extraordinary.

He went down on one knee.

'She's beautiful,' he said huskily, and for one wild moment her heart leapt. Then his head moved to one side, and she saw what he was looking at.

'But she isn't unfinished, is she?' Jago said softly, and Charis shot her grandfather a look so astonished, he immediately shook his head.

No, he seemed to tell her with his eyes. I never told him.

'What do you mean?' the old man asked, looking intently once more at the stranger who seemed to be causing such havoc in his household.

'I mean, she's not unfinished,' Jago insisted. 'Doesn't legend have it that the man who carved this was caught up in a volcano, suffered serious burns, and died before he could finish sculpting it?'

The old man nodded slowly. 'That's the tale told by the old ones, yes,' he confirmed cautiously.

Jago glanced up at him, his face flushed, his eyes gleaming with collector's fever. 'And did you believe it?' he challenged, reading the answer in the old man's eyes. 'No, of course you didn't. Anyone could see that this statue is as it was always meant to be. The carver didn't die – or if he did, he didn't die until he'd finished it. Until it was done.'

'But how can you say that?' the old man asked, determined to play devil's advocate. 'You can see for yourself that the carving stops three-quarters of the way down the rock.'

Charis, hardly daring to breathe, moved forward, getting a better view for herself, until now all three of them were staring at the statue.

It was about two feet tall, the black magma smooth in places, rough and knobbly in others. It looked, somehow, almost red. But so red it was black. For all the years, growing up, that she had gazed at the statue, Charis had never been sure whether it was incredibly dark red, or just black.

But what was not in doubt was the beauty and magnificence of the figure in the carving. A young girl seemed to be struggling up out of the rock, her locks of hair lava flows, her fingers erupting fiery geysers, her neck emerging from a volcanic crater, her face an exquisite mixture of death and life, beauty and ferocity.

And, halfway down, the statue became nothing but rock. If you looked and looked and looked you might picture in your mind's eye how the artist had meant to continue down, showing the rest of the voluptuous female form. But there was nothing but uncut, unshaped rock.

It was her grandfather who'd first asked her if she thought the statue was finished, when she'd been about eleven. And she'd replied, astonished, that, no, of course it wasn't finished. The man who'd carved it had suffered Pele's wrath and died for his pains. For a year she'd thought nothing more of it, until, on her thirteenth birthday, as her body had begun to stir with the first signs of puberty, she'd looked at the statue and suddenly seen it as whole.

For this was not a statue of Pele, the goddess formed and made. This was a statue which depicted the *birth* of Pele. The erupting volcano spewing her forth from its womb. Where the sculptor had carved her lovely face, she was. Where the rock was, the mountain was. As yet unformed but just waiting to form her lower limbs and her dainty feet.

She'd run to her grandfather, so excited by her sudden

discovery, and he'd been pleased, and told her the family secret. For generations, all the royal line had believed the statue to be complete. Only the *malahinis* – the strangers – who came to admire it thought it unfinished.

It had been like a precious family heirloom, separate of the statue itself, this knowledge that only they held.

But now this man, this man of all men, was saying the same thing. How had he seen it? Why him, out of all the art experts, sculpture lovers, craven-eyed collectors and would-be buyers who'd studied it? Why did Jago Marsh see its secret?

'It's not for sale,' Charis said, her voice as hard as a whiplash, almost strident in her determination to make him understand.

Jago stood up and whipped around, confronted, it seemed to him for one confused moment, by the human reincarnation of the stone-hearted woman he'd just been looking at. For a second, in the tight, furious look on her face, he saw the fiery death in Pele's magma face. In the dark chocolate depths of Charis's flashing eyes, he could see the dark red depths he was sure was in the rock.

Then he shook his head. No. No. He was giving her far too much power.

'Everything's for sale,' he said harshly.

'Not her,' Charis said, striding to the statue, feeling the rock, warm and seemingly approving in her hand, before putting it back into the cabinet and firmly turning the key. 'Not as part of a business deal, not for all the tea in China.' She turned back to face the two men.

'Grandfather, it's time for your warfarin. Mr Marsh, I'd like you to leave now.'

Her cool words stirred the air between them, and Jago stared at her, his hands curling and uncurling into fists by his side. She could almost feel him vibrating, but whether in fury, frustration or desire, she couldn't have said.

'All right,' Jago gritted. He took a few steps towards the door, then turned to look at her. He couldn't *not* have taken one final look at her if his life had depended on it.

She was so compelling. And something about her demanded his attention, as if by right. It was as if some unknown thing inside himself seemed to recognize something kindred inside of her.

He didn't like it. In fact, it gave him a curiously vulnerable feeling, which he didn't like one little bit.

But he was not about to back away from it.

'But this isn't goodbye, Charis,' he warned. Oh no. This was a long way from over.

Her eyes seemed to flicker, just for a moment, and then her face became shuttered once more.

Later, when the house was silent, a figure crept from beneath the stairs, stretched, and made its way to the library. A heavy book, wrapped in a discarded napkin, cracked the glass in the library cabinet. Quickly, sure that a silent alarm was probably already ringing at the local police station, the figure grabbed the statue and fled.

There was no doubt at all about the alarm which sounded as the French door was broken open, but by the time the butler raced into the room, the figure was long gone.

And so was the *Heart of Fire*.

Chapter Six

Charis smiled sweetly at the receptionist, and held out a long brown envelope. She was careful to keep her hand steady, although her whole body was shaking so hard with fury, she felt sure that it must be making the reception desk at the Hawaiian Naniloa Hotel rock on its foundations too.

But the receptionist, a pretty girl with a large orchid in her hair, didn't seem to notice.

'This is for Mr Marsh,' Charis said, unnecessarily, for she'd already written his name with a large felt-tip pen on the front. 'It's important he receives it today.'

When she'd woken in the night to the sound of the alarm, she'd instantly dressed and raced downstairs, only to find their butler coming from the library, his normally placid face deeply distressed. And before he even opened his mouth, Charis had known what he was going to say. In a house full of silver, precious objets d'art and worthwhile paintings, she'd instinctively known what had been taken.

She could almost feel the absence of Pele's statue from the house.

The night had been something of a nightmare for her – her grandfather had had to be told and appeased, the police called, then the insurance notified. And all the time she dealt with this, as the dawn filled the sky with colour and the oma'os, Hawaiian's native thrushes, sang outside in the mella bushes, she'd known who was responsible. And yet, when the police had arrived in the form of a relatively high-up official for such a simple burglary (but given the address and occupants concerned, perhaps not surprising), she'd never spoken his name aloud.

She'd told herself that she had no proof it was Jago. That she could be laying herself open to an allegation of slander, even, if she accused him publicly. But even as she told them about the party and agreed to get a guest list from her social secretary, whilst the police would look into the catering and domestic staff, she knew they'd be wasting their time.

It was Jago Marsh who had stolen the *Heart of Fire*. Who else could it be? She knew none of the household servants would do such a thing, and the catering service she'd used had an excellent reputation. And as for the idea of one of her guests stealing it – the idea was absurd. Why would the mayor, or a famous baseball star, or the wife of an ex-governor general, or a doctor in volcanology, or any of the other myriad A-list party-goers, risk such a thing?

No. It was Jago. It had to be Jago. He'd practically told her, when she'd insisted the statue wasn't for sale, that this wasn't the end of it.

So when the police had left, she knew it was up to her to get the statue back herself. Her grandfather was anxious that there be no adverse publicity, and the police had promised to be discreet, but Charis knew that unless she could get it back quickly and quietly, it was bound to leak out to the press. And that thought was like a burr in her side. The *Heart of Fire* had been in her family for generations. They were its guardians, and everyone, especially the older, more traditional islanders, expected them to keep the precious statue safe.

To think that it had been stolen from her home, and right under her nose, made her burn with shame.

The moment the last of the visitors – an insurance assessor – had left, she'd run to her car, a small little economic hatchback, and picked up her mobile phone.

Lehai had been surprised to hear from her boss on a Sunday morning, but did indeed remember where Jago Marsh was staying.

Careful to keep a control on herself, and her driving, Charis had managed to drive at a stately forty miles an hour into the capital city, and on to the outskirts of Hilo Bay. She'd found, amazingly enough, a parking space on Banyan Drive, overlooking Kalaniana Ole Avenue, and by the time she'd walked into the hotel's lobby, thought she had herself fully under control.

She was certainly thinking straight by then. She knew if she rushed up, all hot and bothered, and demanded to know Jago Marsh's room number that, Princess Charis Mina Scott or not, the receptionist would refuse to give it out. So she'd been clever. Reaching into her glove compartment, which was packed with all sorts including some spare stationery and a pen, she'd made out a blank envelope.

Now, handing it over, she managed another smile, hoping her sleepless night wasn't showing. The last thing she wanted was to start the other woman speculating. But she needn't have worried. She'd brushed her hair into vigorus raven waves, and a light application of Princess Mina make-up hid any signs of dark circles under her eyes. She was dressed in a cream two-piece suit and high heels, and had Gucci accessories.

She looked every inch what she was.

'Thank you.' The receptionist took the envelope without batting an eyelid. 'I'll see Mr Marsh receives it.'

Charis nodded and turned away, but after a few steps glanced quickly back, feeling smug as her ruse worked. The receptionist put the envelope in the slot marked PH/14.

Charis grimaced. Trust Jago to have one of the top floor's most luxurious rooms. No doubt it had a view over the harbour along with its own balcony and hotel butler to cater to his every whim.

At least he was still here. She'd half expected to hear that he'd checked out in the middle of the night. No doubt he would have, had he been able to get a flight.

She turned, ostensibly towards the ladies' room, checked that she wasn't being observed, and quickly moved to the stairs.

The hotel, like many buildings in Hilo, wasn't that tall. Since the devastating tsunami of 1960 all but flattened the city, tall buildings had simply never been popular again, and many visitors were surprised by its almost 'primitive' air. Unlike the other island's capital cities, such as Oahu, there wasn't the frenetic nightlife or major shopping centres people had come to associate with a major tourist destination.

But she wasn't in the mood for introspection as she walked up the stairs, her blood pounding in her veins, her heavy breathing having little to do with the exercise she was doing. She emerged on to the top floor like a dynamo, and stalking to his door, began pounding on it viciously.

Inside, Jago was sitting on the balcony with the *Hawaiian Herald*, and a breakfast platter consisting of Kona coffee, French-style croissants and a plateful of fruit, only some of which he recognized – mangoes, passion fruit, wild pomelos, guavas and mountain apples among them.

The sudden, rude pounding made him spill a little coffee onto his newspaper, and cursing, he got up and strode to the door. He'd forsaken the use of a private butler on arrival, as being waited on by a servant still made him feel uneasy. Oh, he'd hired a couple of daily women to help his mother keep the big house in Windsor under control, but butlers were not something he was keen on.

Consequently, when he flung open the door in person, Charis was immediately confronted by a pair of stormy grey eyes.

'Do you have to make that infernal racket?' Jago growled, somehow not surprised to see Charis on the other side of the door. Subconsciously, he supposed, he knew that only Charis could announce herself with such inimitable panache.

She stormed past him, somehow registering the fact that he was dressed in ultra-thin white slacks which seemed to cling to the muscular contours of his thighs, and a dark blue shirt, unbuttoned practically to his navel, revealing a near hairless but well-formed chest. Through the thin dark blue material, she could clearly see the outline of his nipples, and wondered why she should notice such things at all, especially at a time like this. Was she going insane?

'Where is it?' she said flatly, coming to a halt in the middle of the room, and crossing her arms combatively across her chest. One foot tapped impatiently against the expensive Aubusson carpet.

Jago slowly closed the door behind her and contemplated her warily. 'And good morning to you too,' he said facetiously.

Charis sighed elaborately. 'Come on, give it to me,' she snapped, holding out her hand imperiously.

Jago's eyebrow disappeared into his hairline. He smiled

slowly. 'I'd be delighted to give it to you,' he said softly, walking purposely towards her. He grinned when her fulminating expression wavered and became alarmed. Then an unmistakable look of real fury crossed her face, and he felt all sense of amusement flee.

'What's put you in such a tizzy?' he snapped, almost accusingly.

Charis snarled. 'Don't come the innocent act with me, Jago Marsh,' she snapped. 'Look. I'll make you a deal,' she said, trying to be reasonable. Although the big oaf hardly deserved it. 'You give it back, right here and now, and I'll tell the police there's been a mistake. I give you my word, I won't prosecute. Providing you hand it over right now.'

Jago blinked. Police? Prosecute? Had the woman flipped her lovely little lid entirely? To begin with, he'd been amused by this whirlwind visit, but he was beginning to get the nasty feeling that the situation wasn't as amusing as he'd have liked.

For her part, Charis didn't like the look in his eyes one little bit. Because he was looking genuinely puzzled. Wary, even. And it wasn't the reaction she was expecting. If he'd sneered, bluffed or even become threatening, she'd have felt – perversely – much better about things.

Jago came a few steps closer, looking at her. His eyes narrowed. 'You look tired. Overdid the partying, did you? Drink a bit too much punch?'

Charis closed her eyes, heaved a sigh, and then opened them again in a show of exaggerated patience. 'Let's not play games, shall we?' she said, her anger seeming to leach out of her just when she needed it most, leaving her feeling oddly deflated. 'The statue was stolen last night. I want it back,' she finished flatly.

Jago tensed. The *Heart of Fire* was gone? Damn it, now he'd never get his hands on it. Unless he could track it down. It would have been a professional 'hit', of course, for it was too famous and well known to be sold, or rather 'fenced', in the usual way. No, it must have been commissioned. Some collectors, he knew, hired thieves to acquire otherwise unattainable objects as casually as he ordered his shirts from Turnbulls.

Then, as he saw her outstretched hands, her hard, uncompromising face, he felt the blood drain from his face.

She thought he'd stolen it! Of all the damn gall!

Jago took another step towards her, and this time she literally stumbled back.

Charis had seen the stunned surprise hit him like a physical wave, draining his face of all colour. It had been easy, then, to recognize the fury which took over. And for the first time, she'd wondered, actually seriously wondered, if Jago hadn't taken it at all. But surely she couldn't be so wrong?

Then all thought fled and sheer instinct took over, as she realized he was bearing down on her with all the speed and determination of a striking leopard.

'Jago,' she squealed, then gasped as she felt two hard hands grasp her upper arms, bruising her, pulling her forward. Through a moment of stark fear, she was fascinated to see that the scar on his face, rather than being white and standing out, was now the darkest thing on his face. She'd heard the phrase 'going white with fury' before, but had never seen it demonstrated so devastatingly until now. Only his eyes, stormy grey sea, hardened steel eyes, blazed out of his face.

'Are you accusing me of taking your damned statue?' he gritted softly. Expecting him to bellow, the very softness of his voice froze her marrow.

Charis stared at him, mesmerized, unable to say a thing.

She'd never been the cause of so much masculine fury before, and she had no idea how to react to it. She was aware, vaguely, of her heart pounding in equal quantities of fear and excitement. Her brain, also, seemed torn between horror and gratification. Even her insides churned with a confusing mixture of adrenaline and something far softer, warmer, and somehow utterly feminine in character.

She was appalled. And delighted.

As she continued to stare at him mutely, her big, dark chocolate eyes huge in her heart-shaped face, Jago gave her a little shake – just enough to set her wavy raven hair trembling on her shoulders and down her back, like liquid silk.

'Well?' he roared.

Charis swallowed. Her chin angled upwards. And he saw fire, red-hot, like the dark, dark redness in the Pele statue, deepen in her eyes.

'Who else?' she finally got up the courage to spit.

Jago took a huge breath. Who else indeed? Looking at it from her point of view, he could easily see why she should come charging into his room to accuse him. Last night things had got a little out of hand – even he was prepared to admit that.

But he knew something she didn't. Namely, that he *hadn't* stolen the statue. So the question was, indeed, who else?

And, just as she'd reasoned to herself that morning, he too came up with a blank. Servants? Unlikely. Weren't they supposed to be fanatically loyal? The guests?

Or . . . His eyes narrowed as a sudden idea, an extremely nasty and ugly idea, raised its suspicious head. 'Was it insured?' he asked softly.

Charis shrugged her arms, vainly trying to dislodge his grip, but it only made his fingers tighten warningly deeper.

She bit her lip, refusing to cry out, and sighed. 'Yes it was insured,' she admitted wearily. 'But that's not the point. Mere money can't take the place of the *Heart of Fire*. That statue is unique, its importance to the island immeasurable.'

Jago nodded. 'So you say. Tell me, Charis, what made you decide to sell the Princess Mina range in the first place? Getting bored with it, were you? Was it becoming a drag? Had the novelty of playing Little Miss Businesswoman worn off?'

Charis gasped. 'No! How dare you? If you must know, I *had* to sell. The palace is suffering from subsidence and then we suffered some storm damage last winter and the whole roof needs replacing. Normally, we have enough money coming in from stocks and bonds to cover it, but this time the estimates were so high I decided to sell the range. Why are you nodding your head like that and looking so smug?' she finished angrily.

'Oh, just thinking. You need money. You're insured. Your most famous, priceless heirloom mysteriously disappears after you hold a party. Put it all together, and what have you got?'

Although it sounded reasonable, even as he was saying it, Charis began looking at him as if he'd just taken a knife and slid it into her heart, and he found himself unable to believe in his own words. Try as he might, he just couldn't see her as the type to pull some kind of insurance swindle. For one thing, she was far too genuinely concerned with her family's precious reputation.

'You, you, you . . . appalling *monster!*' she finally spat out. 'Let go of me before I *do* call the police. I'll have you up on a charge of assault in an instant, you, you *horrible* man!' Her voice was raised to a near scream by the time she'd finished spluttering.

The vision she had of him then, having to empty his pockets, of being led into a prison cell, of being relieved of his shoelaces and belt, all the time flushed with humiliation and chagrin, was so sweet she could almost feel herself reaching for a telephone and dialling the police.

'You'll soon find out that my family still has some influence in this town. They'll throw the book at you!'

Perhaps they'd even throw him into solitary, where he'd prowl like a caged tiger alternately cursing her name and then begging her for help. So engrossed was she in this wonderful fantasy that when he spoke, she almost didn't take in his actual words.

'In that case,' Jago snarled, 'I might as well be hung for a sheep as for a lamb.'

'Wh-aat?' she wailed and then could say nothing more, for his lips were fastened on hers. She kicked him hard on the shin and felt his lips jerk over hers as he gave an involuntary yelp, but then she was being pulled off the floor, into his arms, lifted so high into the air she was practically leaning against his shoulders. Her hair fell down like a curtain around their faces, blocking out the sunlight and hiding their profiles from anybody who might have been watching.

She tried to breathe, couldn't, drew in a noisy breath through her nostrils, tried to kick him again; she felt him turn sideways, avoiding her kicks, and dug her nails hard into his shoulders. She felt one break but knew that, through the thin shirt, it must be hurting him.

Not that he made any sign of it. His arms around her waist seemed to glow with heat, infusing her with an answering fire. Her insides seemed to be melting, her lips fusing with his. Bright red, white, yellow and orange lights seemed to firework against her closed lids, and her hands, somehow, were now in his hair, feverishly running across his scalp, relishing the sensation of the long silky lengths of straw-coloured locks between her fingers.

Jago moaned, the sound reverberating through her body, making her breasts swell and start to throb. An ache, bordering somewhere between mental and physical, confused her senses. She felt something behind her, and beneath her. The settee? The floor? She didn't know. Couldn't tell. Didn't care. He was lying on her now, but his weight, instead of crushing her, seemed to reinforce her. She felt his fingers splaying against her breast, and her knees jerked in spasmodic reaction.

He moaned again, a curious catlike mewling which astonished her, until she realized it was coming from her own lips. And only then realized that her mouth was free. But only because he was kissing her throat instead, her ears, her neck, his hands thrusting aside the jacket, seeking the tender hollows in her shoulders.

Charis's eyes snapped open. She was looking at the ceiling. So she was on the floor.

She was on the floor being . . . ravished!

She couldn't believe it.

By Jago Marsh.

By Jago Marsh!

Her eyes feathered closed as his lips found the little spot in the hollow of her neck which made her back arch off the floor.

And then she was shoving him aside, reacting to some voice deep inside her that she couldn't quite decipher, and scrambling to her feet. What would her grandfather say? He was relying on her to get the statue back. Conscious thought seemed to come rushing back now, in a scandalised guilty wail. What would her friends say if they could see her now, rolling about on the floor and all mussed, like a character in a French farce? And damn it all, to make matters so much worse, she wanted to get back down on the floor with him. 'I hate you!' she yelled, getting to her feet and backing away.

Jago, breathing heavily, turned on to his side and stared up at her. His face was flushed, the scar now a stark white line again. His eyes seemed somehow fathomless.

He reached out and caught her ankle, his fingers feeling like fire on her flesh. 'Come here,' he said huskily.

Charis yanked her foot away then suddenly stamped it down again, but he was too quick for her, snatching his hand away in time. With a dangerous curse he sat half upright, and Charis ran to the door.

As she turned back he was getting to his feet, his eyes watching her with the strangest expression.

'You're even worse than your brother!' she spat. 'At least he was only a liar and cheat.'

And with that she yanked open the door and was gone.

At exactly the same moment that Charis Scott, shaken to her core, ran down the corridor of the Hawaiian Naniloa, at another hotel on the other side of the harbour, in the bar of the Dolphin Bay Hotel, Rudy Carter smiled affably and indicated the bartender.

'Let me refresh that drink for you. What are you having? G&T?'

Harris McVie, who'd stopped in for a post-prandial refresher, glanced across at the man who'd just taken the seat next to him in the line of bar stools, and smiled cautiously. 'Thanks very much. Kind of you. Are you staying here?'

Rudy nodded. 'For my sins,' he said with mock boredom. 'I thought I'd pay my brother-in-law a visit whilst he was here on the big island, but he's always busy busy busy.' He sighed again, and cheerfully paid and tipped the bartender as he brought over the drinks. 'For all the sight-seeing he's been able to show me, I might as well have stayed in London. Cheers. Mind, the weather's better here, I'll say that for it.'

Harris nodded and sipped.

'Mind you, I'm a bit worried about him. Riordan, that is. He's studying one of the volcanoes here,' Rudy continued blithely. He'd always been good at drama at school, as had Veronica, and he was feeling rather pleased with his performance so far. He'd been studying the type he wanted to emulate for some time, and he was sure he had the holiday bore off to a tee. He was now just the kind of man who'd launch into the tale of his life at the drop of the hat. He'd already noted the American begin to look at his watch before he'd baited the hook.

Now Harris slowly put his drink down. 'Riordan? You're not talking about Dr Vane, are you? The visiting scientist up at the observatory?'

Rudy feigned a look of delighted astonishment. 'Yes! That's the chap! Don't tell me you know him? Must be true what they say, I guess. About it being a small world.'

Harris McVie nodded. 'It must be,' he said quietly.

Rudy nodded, took a sip of his drink, and sighed. He looked worried. 'I only wish he'd cut back on the old booze a bit,' he muttered, almost to himself.

Harris looked surprised. 'Dr Vane? I hadn't heard that he had an alcohol problem.'

'Oh, he hasn't. Not really. I mean, he handles it well. It's just that at this time of year, you know, it's especially hard.' Seeing the encouraging look on the American's face, he turned to face him on the seat. 'My sister – his wife – died around this time. Blames himself. Well, he *was* driving,' he added, careful to keep the real angst and hatred from his voice now. 'Vee tried to get him to let her drive, but . . .' He shrugged. 'It was tragic. She was only thirty-two.' He sighed and ordered another drink. 'Yep, it's really sad. Course, it's not surprising he should go off the rails every now and then. Mind you, we, the family, that is, are feeling a bit more worried about him than usual. He's working too hard. Well, you know the type,' he gushed on, the harmless, slightly sozzled bore that he was. He pretended not to notice that the American was now sitting up straighter, any look of boredom completely gone from his face. 'Always work, work, work. Booze. Guilt. Not surprising poor ol' Rory's not himself,' Rudy waffled on, sprinkling his venom like pure olive oil. 'Old Gilbert, that's the family doc, thinks he might be heading for a breakdown, but I can't see it myself. Well, I think I'd better hit the beach before all the chairs are gone. Nice speaking to you, old sport.' Rudy raised one hand, smiled amiably, staggered a little from his stool and wandered off.

Harris McVie watched him go, his face thoughtful.

Jago Marsh walked out on to the balcony and stared across the bay. His breathing was back to normal at last, but he still felt restless. Full of energy. Sexual energy.

He threw himself into the chair, which creaked in protest, and cursed. Damn that woman. Coming here to accuse him of theft. Then making him want her. And want her so damned much. And then changing her mind halfway through, and expecting him to like it. And then, to top it all off, throwing out that crack about Keith. And, now that he came to think about it, just what had she meant by *that*?

He'd have to have a word with Keith.

Then he shook his head. First things first. He had to find the *Heart of Fire*. That was the only way he would ever get the

111

chance to buy it, legitimately, off her. And since he had no idea how to go about it, he'd have to find someone who could. But a good private investigator shouldn't be all that hard to find. And once it was located, it would be fair game again. But he'd have to be quick – once the statue was off the island, and buried in some collector's vault, they'd never see it again.

He wanted that statue almost as much as he wanted its owner. Jago snarled and threw that thought aside. Scratch that. That little episode with Charis was just a case of chemistry getting out of hand. It wouldn't happen again. He wouldn't let it. No, he'd concentrate instead on getting back the statue. He wanted the pleasure of proving his innocence, and at the same time presenting the statue to her, along with the real culprit, and making her eat crow. He could almost picture it – him handing the statue back, one fire goddess returning to another! Wouldn't she be miffed. Her eyes flashing . . .

He shut his eyes. Damn it, forget about that, he warned himself grimly. So, she'd lit a fire under him. He had it under control now.

Didn't he?

First thing Monday morning, in the office, Lehai, sensing trouble, handed her boss the folder she'd asked for, and beat a hasty retreat.

Charis lifted the telephone and called the number of her biggest competitor in the islands. She was going to sell the Princess Mina range now. As soon as possible. Once it was off her hands, Jago Marsh would have no more excuse for staying on the island.

And she wanted him gone. Out of her life. For good. Big time.

Right?

Chapter Seven

Riordan hesitated briefly outside Naomi's door, raised his fisted hand, hesitated again, then knocked firmly.

His small apartment was one floor below hers, and it was usually their habit for Naomi to come down to him in the mornings, and then for both of them to drive to work in their shared Jeep. So when Naomi opened the door to find him on her doorstep, she knew straight away that the usual routine had been forsaken for some reason.

And when she realized that he was dressed in white slacks and a cheap and cheerful Hawaiian shirt, she felt almost nonplussed, so used was she to seeing him in his working 'uniform'.

'Morning,' Riordan said briefly, his eyes skimming over her figure. She'd just come out of the shower, and was wearing only a T-shirt and her khaki shorts, both of which clung to her damp skin like ardent admirers. Her short fair hair was also damp, and clung to her scalp in spiky whorls, and she felt herself blushing as she realized the picture she must be presenting to him.

'Er, come in,' she said, backing up and allowing him into the apartment. Riordan glanced around as he did so, unsurprised to see that the accommodations were exactly the same as his own, right down to the decor. But then, all holiday/temporary digs were so impersonal.

He supposed the last real home he had was the smart little townhouse which he and Veronica had shared in London. But he'd rented that out soon after his wife's death, preferring a smaller bedsit whenever he was in the capital. Which was hardly ever.

Now, for some reason, he felt a sudden wave of homesickness wash over him. But not for any particular place; it was more like a sudden need to have a home again. It took him off-guard.

'Please, take a seat. I'll just get ready,' Naomi said nervously. 'You're early. Did the office call in?' she asked, talking over her shoulder as she jogged quickly to her bedroom. Just as she was passing through the door, however, Riordan coughed. It was a strangely diffident kind of cough, and it stopped her in her tracks. She looked back at him over one shoulder.

'I thought we'd skive off, for once,' Riordan said, sounding distinctly embarrassed.

Naomi's jaw literally dropped. Skive off? 'You mean,' she said, uncertain that she'd heard him correctly, 'not go into the office?'

Riordan grinned. He couldn't help it. She looked and sounded so gobsmacked. Was he really such a slave-driver? 'That was the meaning of "skive off" when I last checked,' he murmured, eyes twinkling. 'It means to not go to work. To come up with some mendacious excuse to avoid work. To "play hookey", as our American cousins would say. To . . .'

Naomi laughed. 'All right, all right, Riordan, I know what it means,' she said, then cocked her head to one side to consider

114

him more closely. It was a habit of hers to move her head that way, like an inquisitive small dog, and he found it particularly endearing.

'No, I haven't had a brainstorm, if that's what you're thinking,' he said, and she grinned again, liking this new, approachable, human version of Dr Riordan Vane very much.

'Nor been taken over by alien body snatchers?' she felt emboldened to tease.

'Nope, nor have I been brainwashed by an evil genius, or lost my memory. I just thought that it's time we got to see a bit more of the island, besides our own little volcano. It struck me as absurd that we'd had so little time off, and seen so few of the sights. Of course, if you'd rather work—'

'Not on your life,' Naomi grinned. 'Just give me five minutes and I'll be ready.'

So saying, she sprinted into the bedroom, opened her wardrobe door, looked bleakly at the rows of good solid work clothes and selected, from her very meagre choice of leisure wear, a bright blue pair of shorts and a shirt of red, green, blue and gold swirls. She quickly towel-dried her hair and brushed the short silken silvery strands into an attractive halo around her head, then raced to her vanity table. Her make-up supply was almost as poor as her wardrobe, but she added a quick dash of red lipstick and the very last squirt from a bottle of Yves St Laurent perfume, which her mother had bought for her for the Christmas before last.

She made a severe mental note to herself to go shopping – soon.

When she appeared at the doorway, Riordan was prowling around like a caged lion, and he turned eagerly towards her when he sensed movement. His eyes darkened. She looked so young and bright and vibrant, and so unlike the khaki-clad assistant of all those years before, he was again taken off-guard.

What was happening to him?

'So, what's on the itinerary for today?' she asked brightly, perhaps sensing that if she didn't step into the breach, and quick, he might change his mind. He had that dithering look some men had when they weren't too sure of themselves. It was not a look that she'd ever thought to see on Riordan Vane's face. The super-scientist. The most revered of volcanologists. The cold, calm, equivocal Ph.D.

She liked it.

Riordan blinked. 'I don't know,' he said, feeling stupid. 'I hadn't actually given that a thought. Isn't there some "must see" place on the island? You know, if you're in Paris you have to see the Eiffel Tower. In Rome, the Coliseum. Isn't there a place like that here?'

He's babbling, Naomi thought, careful to keep her delighted surprise from showing. Good grief, the man she'd fallen in love with was human after all.

'I don't think so,' she said casually, more than willing to take the strain off him. In fact, she would have been willing to die for him, right at that moment, for she was all too aware of what all this was costing him. *Must* be costing him. He'd built up a very stable wall around him and his enclosed little world, and now he was deliberately knocking holes in it.

And all for her, she hoped.

Oh, how she prayed.

But even if life played the cruellest of tricks on her, and it turned out that she wouldn't be the one to reap the ultimate benefit of his return to life, she would do anything to help him achieve it. Because he needed to live again. He *deserved* to.

'Why don't we pick up some brochures from the lobby downstairs and decide what we like best?' she asked cheerfully, even though her heart ached slightly.

Riordan looked relieved. 'OK,' he agreed, and wondered why she bothered with him. He was so damned useless at this kind of thing.

They rather liked the look of the Lyman House Memorial Museum, which promised to offer a fascinating collection on the island's ethnic and major ethnic immigrants cultures, but Naomi gently vetoed that. She didn't want the word 'educational' to feature anywhere in their day's activities.

Some of the driving tours promised spectacular scenery but she didn't want to spend too much precious time in the car. One of them would have to drive, and she wanted to be able to concentrate on him totally. And have him concentrate on her. Now that he'd made the first tentative moves, she wasn't about to allow any backsliding.

So they decided to pick a beach. A few hours in the sun, watching the surfers and paragliders, eating ice cream and just talking appealed to Naomi more than any Eiffel Tower or ancient Roman amphitheatre.

There were plenty of beaches to choose from, including Spenser Beach, Green Sand, Hapuna and the Kona State Park, but they opted to stay local and headed out for the Honolii Beach Park, driving just a few miles from the capital.

The beach was everything a travel agent could want to put on a poster, with black sand for that touch of the unusual, but with the more traditional turquoise seas, swaying coconut palms and pristine rainforests abutting it. The rainiest season, which in Hawaii was between December and February, was long gone, and the temperature was a bearable seventy-six degrees or so. Or so the electronic temperature gauge stated on one of the buildings they passed by.

They found a few sun loungers under the shade of a coconut palm, and bought a fruit crush from a mobile vendor, a cheerful Japanese who took a great interest in Naomi's legs.

Riordan noticed.

And Naomi noticed Riordan notice.

As she took the drink Riordan handed her, she smiled widely. Riordan grinned self-mockingly, shook his head, and waved off the vendor, who was trying to sell them on the idea of an ice-cream cone.

The beach was not particularly big, nor was it particularly deserted. Naomi glanced out to the swelling waves of the mighty Pacific Ocean and sighed. Gulls cried mournfully overhead but nothing could break the spell of the moment.

'I suppose your boyfriend back home wouldn't approve of our ice-cream man, had he been here,' Riordan said, then shook his head at himself again, this time for real.

Clumsy. Very, very clumsy.

But hell, how long was it since he'd dated? If this was even a date? No wonder he was all at sea. But how else was he going to find out if Naomi was taken? He'd never heard her talk about a man, but then, he'd never encouraged personal chit-chat in the lab.

He dunked his head and took a gulp of ice-cold pineapple juice, and hoped he didn't look as uncomfortable as he felt.

Naomi drank from her own cup placidly. 'I don't have a man back home,' she said, calmly and clearly.

Riordan nodded. Now what? Did he even know what he *wanted* to happen next? In fact, what was he even doing here in the first place?

He'd woken up that morning, for the first time ever, wanting to do something more than get up and go to work. And namely to spend some time alone with his research assistant.

No. With *Naomi*. Somehow, Naomi and his research assistant had become two separate people. Now when had that happened?

But he knew, of course. It was the night he'd danced with her. It had all started to go wrong then. Or go right then. He wasn't sure which it was.

He sighed and rubbed a hand through his hair. 'I'm not very good at this, am I?' he said, and turned to her quickly in surprise as she said softly, 'No, you're not.' And then, looking at him openly, shrugged and said, 'But then neither am I. So what?'

Riordan grinned and felt himself relaxing. After all, it wasn't a matter of life and death, was it? 'Yeah,' he said softly. 'So what.' He glanced out over the ocean and said, 'Can you swim?'

Naomi shook her head.

'Me neither,' he said. 'So that's one thing we have in common. Shall we see if we can find another?'

Naomi leaned sideways on her sun lounger, her eyes bright with everything which was good in life. 'Let's,' she said.

Two hours later, they knew each other's life history. Or at least, as much of it as each felt comfortable telling the other in this tenuous, delicate, first stage of their courtship.

And they had indeed found many other things in common, including a well-hidden love of country and western music, an openly admitted preference for classic murder mysteries, with Agatha Christie and Ngaoi Marsh battling it out for first place amongst the honours, with Dorothy L. Sayers, Patricia Wentworth and all the others jostling for a mention.

They'd also found they could laugh without embarrassment in each other's presence, that Naomi didn't feel the need to keep checking that her lipstick hadn't smudged off (a usual worry on one of her rare forays into dating) and, on Riordan's part, that he could talk even about Veronica.

True, he'd kept strictly to the facts as the outside world thought they knew them, but for the first time ever he could talk about his marriage to another person.

Even if he lied.

After lunching on macadamia nuts, eggs, saimin (a delicious kind of noodle soup) and lomi salmon, they headed for the Liliuokalani Gardens. As they parked and walked into the entrance, Naomi reached out and took his hand.

After their morning confidences, she felt almost safe doing so, and when he glanced down in surprise, she was able to meet his gaze without either flinching or looking defiantly bold. For a reward, she felt his fingers squeeze hers warmly.

The gardens were lovely, with an ornamental Japanese style predominating.

'So, what made you apply to my team once you'd got your doctorate?' Riordan asked, as they crossed one of the many slender foot bridges and paused to admire the beauty of what looked like a Japanese acer.

Naomi smiled. 'Hardly a difficult choice. You're the best. I wanted to work with the best.'

'Is that flattery?'

'No. Just the truth.'

Riordan frowned down thoughtfully into a brightly pink mass of flowers. 'And did I measure up to expectations?' he asked gruffly.

Naomi, sensing trouble, quickly sifted through her options, and decided on the truth. 'Yes.'

Riordan sighed and looked away. So he was a big man in

her eyes. He wasn't sure that he liked that.

'Let's see what's so blue through there,' he said, and pointed off to their left. Knowing this particular conversation was far from over, and that at some point she'd have to find out what had made him so tense again, she followed him, making a small sound of pleasure as they rounded a path and found themselves facing Coconut Island. It was a mere green speck in the bay, and a quick glimpse at the brochure she'd brought with her, told her that the island used to be called Mokuola, or 'Healing Island'.

'Apparently, it's a *pu'uhonua*, or place of refuge,' she read out loud, looking up at the small speck of green and imagining canoeing out there and never having to worry about the world you left behind. To have a place where nothing could get you. Then she glanced down and read again, and sighed heavily. There had also been a luakini there, it seemed, where human sacrifices were made by dropping an enormous stone on to the chest of the sacrifice, who was bound to a rock.

'There's always something,' Riordan said, making her jump, as she hadn't realized he'd been reading over her shoulder. 'Even here in paradise, there's always something.' His voice was ineffably sad.

Naomi caught her breath. There it was. The perfect opportunity to say what she knew must be said.

'So what's your serpent in paradise, Riordan?' she asked, so softly the trade wind seemed to snatch it away before it left her lips.

But he'd heard.

'My wife. Veronica,' he said. And it seemed to have been dragged from some deep dark part of him, so deep and dark that the trade wind didn't want anything to do with it, and Naomi heard it loud and clear.

Of course. The old enemy. The lovely, unbeatable, dead Veronica. How had she ever thought she could compete? Even now, six years after her death. Even now, when Riordan seemed, at last, willing to live again, if not to love. Fool. To think that she would be the one who could unchain him from Veronica.

And yet . . . she had to try.

'You loved her so much?' she asked forlornly.

Riordan blinked and looked at her quickly. His eyes looked astounded for a moment, and when Naomi, at last, could look at him, a vestige of that astonishment still remained.

He saw the look of shock in her eyes and quickly turned away. 'I loved Veronica when I married her,' he said flatly. And then turned away. He'd bared enough of his soul for one day. 'Come on, I want to take a look at the Wailuku Falls.'

Naomi, under other circumstances, would have been enchanted with the Wailuku river and the waterfalls, the river being one of the longest on the Hawaiian archipelago.

But his last words in the gardens still haunted her.

What had he meant by it? He loved her when he married her? Well, of course he had – why did people marry except for love? Occasionally for money, perhaps, but that would never apply with a man like Riordan.

So did it mean . . . could it possibly mean . . . that he didn't love her later? It seemed to be what his words implied. But where did that leave her?

Riordan Vane had been in obvious mourning ever since Veronica's death. It was well known that he hadn't even looked at another woman. He went around looking as shuttered as a villa in a hurricane, as walled off from the world as any medieval monk in his monastery.

122

Why did a man do that to himself, if not for love?

A tour guide, with a gaggle of wide-eyed tourists, jostled past them, and his words washed uncaringly over her. 'This river, which means "destroying water" has a ferocious reputation during high rain, but of course we needn't worry about that today!'

Somebody laughed in mock relief.

The world kept on turning, as it always did, and Naomi sighed.

Ahead of her, a large rocky outcrop, which must have been visible even from the bridge between Puueo and Keawe Streets, was called, so the guide now informed his troop of avid listeners, Maui's Canoe.

Beside her, Riordan was dark and silent, and once again, unknowable. And Naomi wasn't sure where she went from here.

'In legend' – the guide's voice was getting fainter and fainter as Naomi and Riordan lagged behind – 'the mighty warrior Maui abandoned it there after he'd raced back from the island, which still bears his name, to rescue his mother Hina, who was trapped by rising waters in a cave, engineered by a dragon.'

Naomi smiled ruefully, feeling a definite affinity with the mighty warrior. She too sensed that someone she loved was trapped and in danger of drowning. But who was her particular dragon? And how did she slay it?

She'd always thought it was Veronica, beautiful and beloved Veronica. But was it?

'Maui's route is now followed by our own Waianuenue Avenue, which means "Rainbow seen in the water" in Hawaiian,' the guide's voice, now a mere thread of sound coming from somewhere out of sight, wafted back to them.

Up ahead, she could just begin to hear the sound of the waterfall. Wordlessly, she kept on walking by the man beside her. She couldn't have reached and taken his hand now if her life had depended on it.

Riordan, too, was lost in thought, but his mind was on a night, long, long ago, it seemed now. A night far removed from the balmy, sultry nights they had here. A night of cold English rain. A night when he had killed his wife.

Up ahead, Naomi saw the waterfall at last – a broad waterfall, with Mauna Kea looming high in the background, its summit still snow-capped. But for once, the sight of a volcano refused to move her. She looked at Riordan, who also looked at the volcano with unseeing eyes.

How did she reach him?

Two trails led around the waterfall, neither of them allowing visitors to get too close. But off to the left she saw a small staircase. It looked muddy and slippery and the guide, who was leading his group away now, obviously had no intention of letting them climb it.

'Let's see what's up there,' Naomi said, breaking the silence.

Wordlessly, Riordan nodded, holding her elbow as they negotiated the tricky stairs then instantly letting her go once they'd reach the top.

What met them was a view which drew level with the stream bed at the top of the falls. It was a dank, warm, noisy but utterly private spot, and Naomi had a rare sense of enchantment.

'It's lovely here,' she said dreamily.

Riordan also, seemed to be affected by it. 'Yes. It is,' he said quietly. A Japanese white-eye chirruped from a bush above them, as if making the vote unanimous.

Riordan leaned forward on the wooden railing, staring

down into the water.

At last he spoke. 'Don't love me,' he said. 'I'm not worth it.'

Naomi froze for an instant, then leaned on the railing beside him, and in the water saw a tiny fish dart amongst the pebbles.

'Too late,' she said softly. 'I've loved you for years.'

Riordan sighed heavily and turned his head. She turned hers. Eyes met, blue on blue.

He moved towards her, so infinitely slowly, that with the motion of water in her peripheral vision, and the rushing sound of it all around her, it was hard for her to tell he was moving at all. Only when his lips at last touched hers, feather light, could she be sure she wasn't imagining it.

She kissed him back, lightly, gently, wanting more, much more, but afraid now to take it.

Riordan moved closer, his arm coming around her shoulder, pulling her into his body. Naomi clung to him, her hands flattened against either side of his spine, her palms tingling to the warmth of his body heat through the shirt.

His kiss deepened, but so did his panic.

Abruptly he pulled away, stepping back, shaking his head, the sun giving his thick, nut-brown hair a deep chestnut glow. His eyes, though, were shadowed.

'Why?' Naomi cried, bereft.

She took a step towards him and he turned away. 'You don't understand,' he muttered. 'My wife . . .' His voice trailed away, and Naomi shook her head, bitter tears making everything around her become star-shaped and blurred.

'I'm sorry,' she said. But she didn't know what she was apologizing for. For daring to think she could set him free of his memories, perhaps? For her presumption in thinking she could ever take Veronica's place? For being so stupid as to hope?

'You don't understand,' Riordan said flatly. 'It's no good loving me,' he said helplessly.

Naomi raised her face. A last desperate gamble, instinctive in nature, had words leaving her mouth before she even knew they'd formed in her brain. 'Is it any good loving me?'

Riordan's head whipped around. 'What do you mean?' he asked harshly.

Naomi had no idea what she meant. 'I mean,' she said clearly, 'if I'm not allowed to love you, are you allowed to love me?'

Riordan stared at her. He went very pale. 'I don't know,' he whispered.

Naomi wiped a tear from her face, and her chin came slowly up. 'Well, why don't we find out?' she said.

In a small but neatly appointed office in downtown Hilo, Kalani Ahuna, known simply as 'Kal' to everyone who knew him, put down the telephone receiver and leaned back in his swivel chair.

He was smiling.

And he had reason to smile. Yesterday, he'd just picked up a big fat cheque for Ahuna and Trent, Private Investigations Ltd, from an *haole* bigwig from London, and a few moments ago he'd just confirmed a nice little fact which might prove invaluable in solving his latest case.

His newest commission was also one which appealed to him greatly, and was a far cry from his usual divorce cases and industrial espionage forays. In fact, it was very much like something out of *The Maltese Falcon*, Kal thought now with a grin.

Find a missing rare artefact.

But Kal knew himself to be nothing like Philip Marlowe or

Sam Spade, and it was because of his excellent reputation for knowledge of computers in all their many forms, plus his network of willing spies, which had led Mr Jago Marsh to his door.

When he'd told him the famous *Heart of Fire* had been stolen, he'd wondered, briefly, if his client was mad. He'd looked rich, sane and serious, though, and he'd accepted the advance with no problem at all.

And he'd only needed to make a few phone calls and tap away on his computer keys to find out that Jago Marsh was as sane as they came. A few more bribes to a few more willing spies confirmed that, yes, indeed, something serious had happened on the night of Charis Scott's party for her grand-father.

Now he knew something else.

At the party that night had been a well-known (but harm-less) kleptomaniac, a wealthy Australian matron whose embarrassed family inevitably returned stolen items and paid for any inconvenience, one serious collector of ancient statu-ary and now, one Randolf Voight Carter the III, whom nobody had seen leave that night.

The phone call he'd just received was from the last of the catering staff he'd tracked down, who'd confirmed that he remembered the Englishman, but that, no, he hadn't seen him leave that night either.

Nor had any of the valet parking people, or night staff on duty that night.

Kal added the name to the list.

Jago Marsh was paying him big money to find the thief and the statue. The *Heart of Fire*. Like all Hawaiians, he'd heard of it, and knew it to be a carving of the fire goddess Pele. Legend had it that any erupting volcano would always flow away from where the statue was, thus saving whatever village or town was host to it.

And now someone had pinched it. It irked Kal's sense of patriotism, and he would have tried to find it, even if he wasn't being paid handsomely to do just that.

But it wouldn't hurt to earn that very hefty bonus Jago Marsh had promised him if he could do so within the week!

Kal got up and reached for his hat – a battered straw concoction which was his current favourite.

First stop – the Australian kleptomaniac. After all, you never knew your luck.

Chapter Eight

Jago pulled the big hardback book on Hawaiian mythology a little further up his knees and continued to read avidly.

'Pele's spirit, according to local legend, resides in the Halemaumau crater on the Kilauea volcano. At one time she had a short, violent marriage to Kamapuaa, the god of water. But, in rage, she routed him from their home with streams of lava.'

In the main room beyond the balcony, the television set was on, and although it was approaching the dinner hour, he was far too interested in his book to think about food just yet. Besides, reading was taking his mind off Kal's investigations. So far, he'd reported, the Australian kleptomaniac was out, and he was following up on the other collector, but things weren't looking too good there. It would all be in the report he'd fax over later this evening.

Jago sighed, sipped his drink – some fruit-loaded, tangy concoction which seemed to be a speciality of the hotel – and read some more.

'Described as She-Who-Shapes-The-Sacred-Land in ancient Hawaiian chants, the volcano goddess was passionate, volatile and capricious.'

Jago grinned. Now who did that remind him of? He rubbed his hand, wondering just how it would be feeling now if the little minx had managed to succeed in stomping down on it with her high-heeled shoe.

'Pele was one of the first voyagers to sail to Hawaii, pursued, legends say, by her angry older sister, Na-maka-o-kahai, because Pele had seduced her husband.'

Jago shook his head, tut-tutting mildly. The things fire goddesses did get up to. He drained his drink, closed the book with a snap, and walked into the living room.

He was just unbuttoning his shirt, preparatory to taking a shower and then changing for an evening spent in what passed as Hilo's nightlife, when the television suddenly said her name. He wondered, for one nasty moment, if he was hearing things.

He blinked, turning to the set, and reached for the remote control to turn up the volume on the news item. No, it was definitely about Charis, and suddenly her face filled the screen. Her hair, that wonderful fall of raven locks, was swept back in an ultra-chic French pleat, with plumeria blooms strategically placed down its length. She looked fantastic in an emerald green, severely tailored suit, green eye shadow and glossy plum lipstick. Beside her, a middle-aged man looked like the proverbial cat which had just scoffed a particularly plump canary.

'Tell me, Mr Man'ola, how does it feel to be the new owner of the Princess Mina range?' the reporter, a young woman, gushed with fake enthusiasm.

'Well, naturally, we at Fantasia are over the moon. We've always said that the Princess Mina range was really first class.'

'And there's to be no changing the name of the Princess

Mina range?' the reporter asked coyly, whilst Jago snarled viciously over the other man's more mild reply.

'Of course they won't change the name,' Jago snapped. 'That's the biggest part of its mystique. They paid for the name above anything else.'

He turned off the television set, fuming, and grabbed his keys. A maid, ready to start turning down beds and lay out her nightly flower and attractively wrapped mint, which went on every pillow at night, for once failed to smile and call out cheerfully *'aloha,'* to the passing guest. The man from PH14, she thought sorrowfully to herself instead, looked like he was on his way out to fight a demon. And, from the look on his face, she rather pitied the demon.

Charis was still in the office, exhausted after a day of signing papers, talking to journalists, taping the coverage for the nightly TV news, and generally tying up the 1001 things that needed to be tied up, when you had just sold your entire business.

She now had a huge bank balance, with more than enough to be able to pay the builders to start work on the palace, and still have enough left over to never work again, should she so choose.

But she didn't so choose. The thought of being a lady of leisure, for some reason, didn't appeal. In fact, for a woman who'd just pulled off a nice, if unremarkable, little coup, she felt decidedly flat. Perhaps she'd start something new. Not cosmetics, of course, that was out. But a boutique? Jewellery? There were some very avant garde designers coming out of art colleges nowadays, and surely they were ripe to create a 'Hawaiian' look. Whatever that might be.

Then she nearly jumped out of her skin as the door to her

office swung open so viciously the door slammed into the wall and started to ricochet back, before a fair-haired tornado swept into the room, trailing a frankly terrified-looking Lehai.

'I'm sorry, your highness,' she burbled, obviously very distressed to revert to Charis's title like this, 'but he just came past me . . .'

Charis stood up hastily. Jago Marsh was too tall to face sitting down. Even standing up, and in her best four-inch-high stilettos, he still towered above her.

'It's all right, Lehai,' she managed to squeak, then cleared her throat. Doing mouse interpretations, she realized immediately, looking into his furious grey eyes, was definitely not the way to go here. 'You can leave now,' she said, far more firmly. 'It's been a long day.'

Lehai stared at her unhappily, then transferred her gaze to the rigid back of the man dominating the room. 'Really, you can go,' Charis said. 'Mr Marsh's business won't take long,' she added, even more firmly.

Lehai, still very reluctant, backed out of the room. But she wasn't going to leave her office until the big scary scar-faced Englishman had left. No way. And if she heard her beloved boss screaming, she'd phone the police then come charging in with something hard and heavy!

Jago waited for the door to close, then forced himself to relax. Damn it, he felt as charged as a lightning rod after a thunderstorm. What was it about this woman that managed to push all his buttons?

'Well, you kept your little buy-out to Fantasia very quiet,' he said, his voice ominously quiet and reasonable. 'So quiet, in fact, that we at Marsh Pharmaceuticals never even got wind of it. You might have saved me the trouble of flying all the way out here and—'

'Oh, put a sock in it,' Charis said inelegantly, having the satisfaction, at last, of seeing his jaw go slack in shock. She shuddered to think what her grandfather would say if he could hear her being so vulgar. But, after the day she'd just had, she was definitely in no mood for Jago Marsh's little machinations.

As if he could make her feel guilty. Ha!

'You never had any intention of buying the Princess Mina range,' she went on. 'So why don't you just admit it? All you wanted was to get your hands on the *Heart of Fire*. What did you think you were going to do?' she challenged, placing her hands on her hips like an avenging fury. 'Make a tempting offer, then mention that it was only on the condition that you were given a little perk to go with it? Hmm? That perk being, of course, the option to buy the statue?' She was still wearing her hair in the French pleat, but the emerald green jacket was now draped over the back of her chair, and the top two buttons on her brilliant white blouse were undone. She moved forward, the better to confront him. 'Did you really think that I'd be so droolingly bowled over by the promise of big money from such a flatteringly major world player that I'd be beguiled enough to agree to anything you asked?' she snapped.

Jago dragged in a quick breath. She'd got it so unerringly right that he didn't know whether to applaud or bluff. Either way, it left him with only one way to go.

'As a matter of fact,' he drawled, determined at all costs to hide the fact that she'd just scored a palpable hit, 'the statue was only secondary. But you're quite right,' he said quickly, holding up his hand, as she opened her delectable mouth to let rip again, 'the Princess Mina range wasn't even a consideration. It might be fine for a small, home-town, home-brewed

133

little business, but it would hardly be of much interest to me.'

Well, he couldn't let her get away with too much. He'd never hear the end of it.

Her eyes flashed dangerously.

'No. It was for my brother's sake that I really came,' he said, and saw a look of dumbfounded surprise wash over her. He flushed angrily. 'Yes, Keith,' he growled. 'I know he must come so low down on your list of things to worry your pretty little head over, being such a *princess* and all, but his mother and I are rather fond of him. And when he came back mauled about after your treatment of him, I rather—'

'*Mauled?* My treatment of *him?*' she raged. 'What on earth are you talking about?'

Now it was Jago's turn to put his hands on his hips and look disgusted. Quickly, Charis lowered her own hands and went back to her desk. Though she stood behind her chair, she didn't sit. Instead she looked at him, openly puzzled.

At last, something had finally struck her. Jago Marsh seemed quite genuine in what he was saying. Now that they'd got the Princess Mina thing out of the way once and for all, they were obviously getting to the bottom of what was really worrying him.

Hadn't she, all along, even at their first meeting, sensed that there was some kind of sub-text to him, which she wasn't privy to?

'Yes,' Jago said now, a little less heatedly, as if he too was aware that the battle ground was shifting. 'When you broke your engagement to him and dropped him because—'

'*What?*' she shouted. 'Broke my *what* to him?'

Jago's eyes narrowed. A very nasty feeling indeed was beginning to creep up the back of his spine, making the hairs on his neck rise.

'I was never engaged to your brother,' Charis said, taking such long, deep, agitated breaths that his eyes fell unwillingly to her breasts, pressing hard against the cool white silk of her blouse. He dragged his eyes back to her face quickly, and had to admit she looked genuinely aggrieved.

'He told me that you dumped him when you realized that, as the younger brother of a company privately owned by an older sibling, any heirs were likely to be my own children, and not his.'

Charis gaped at him. It was the only way he could describe it.

Feeling less and less sure of his ground, Jago nevertheless had no choice but to plug on. 'Apparently, a younger son wasn't any good to a princess with a palace to maintain and royal jewels to procure. So you dumped him.' That hadn't, of course, been exactly how Keith had described it, but he'd been able to read between the lines all right.

Charis did sit down now. Heavily. She looked at him incredulously.

'*And you believed him?*' she finally said, no force at all in her voice now. This was worse, far worse, than she'd ever thought. The woman Jago was describing was a monster. And yet, she thought fairly, how many women did she know who thought money and status were the only things worth having, fighting and cheating for? How many of her acquaintances *would* in fact have dumped Keith for being less than needed? She could name at least three.

No, it wasn't surprising, perhaps, that Jago Marsh had probably had experience of fortune hunters before.

It was only surprising – no, extremely, hideously *hurtful* – that he should think she was one of them.

She could feel her heart actually aching that he should

think so. She looked at him, but as she did so, the desire to jump to her own defence withered and died. Pride, at last, took a hand, driving away the pain and replacing it with self-righteous anger.

Far easier to deal with.

'Oh, get out,' she said, the disgust in her voice enough to make him actually flinch. 'I've had it with you Marsh men. You're both as bad as each other.'

Not true, of course. After finding out what Keith Marsh had been up to, she'd just dismissed him with barely a wince and never another thought. But this man, she knew, after he'd gone and she'd had a chance to calm down, was going to leave a great big rent in the fabric of her life.

She just knew he was. She could feel it, already forming.

'Well,' she snapped, raising her head and giving him daggers. 'Are you still here?'

Jago had never been talked to in that tone of voice before, with such venomous yet weary disgust. Such disappointment, overlaid with contempt. He had no idea how to react to it.

Surprisingly, he didn't feel angry. Perhaps, because, subconsciously at least, he was beginning to feel as if he might not just deserve it.

One thing was for sure – he was going to pin Keith down and have it out with him once and for all. But right now, he had another, bigger problem.

He felt like a prize bastard.

He'd hurt her, he knew that. This was no play-acting on her part. No female hysteria, designed to make him feel guilty. He'd caused her pain.

And he didn't like it.

'Charis,' he said softly.

Her head shot up. Fire spit from her eyes and he shook his

head. Obviously, this was not the time for soft words and olive branches.

He turned and walked away.

Charis watched him go, her mind imprinted with his image. His eyes, for once, had looked gentle – the grey of a dove's plumage instead of an icy, northern sea. The lines of his face, even around the white line of his scar, had been, for once, relaxed and at rest. Even his mouth had looked tender.

Why, she thought deploringly, hadn't she let him speak? What might he have said? Had she just ruined her life for ever?

She wanted to laugh at herself for the last thought. It was so absurdly dramatic. Who did she think she was – a modern-day Juliet? Well, of course she wasn't about to take poison. Or throw herself into a volcano or the deep blue sea. She'd be all right.

He'd go. And she'd find another man. Of course she would.

But she couldn't quite convince herself. Somehow, try as she might to shake it off, she couldn't believe that she hadn't just made the biggest mistake of her life.

Would it have cost her so much to just listen to him? a persistent little voice whined in the back of her head. Obviously his younger brother, the worthless little toe-rag, had fed him a line. Was it so unforgivable for an older brother to believe him?

So he'd stolen the *Heart of Fire*. Probably. But maybe not.

Charis slowly lowered her head on to her arms and began to sob.

Everything was such a mess. Such a big, ugly, painful mess.

Outside, Jago climbed into his car and sat staring up at a big banyan tree sightlessly. He felt as if he'd just been put through an emotional wringer.

And he didn't like it.

How had he let her get under his skin like this?

And how the hell did he get her out again? He slammed the car into gear and roared away.

On the western elevation of Mount Kulahaleha, the ground rumbled, but coquettishly, like a kitten about to pounce on a small soft toy. It sent no more than a few loose pebbles and some trickles of top soil skittering down a few metres to rest against some boulders.

But Riordan heard it, and Naomi, who was kneeling at the time, checking a ground temperature gauge, felt it. It seemed to shiver up her knee like a small electric shock and she rose, looking across at Riordan quickly, having no need to ask out loud the question.

Did you feel that?

Wordlessly, Riordan nodded back. *Yes.*

'I wonder what it registered back at the lab. Enough to get on the Richter scale?' she asked calmly.

Riordan shook his head. 'I doubt it,' he said. She believed him. He had a feel for things like this.

She wrote down the temperature reading, and frowned. 'Riordan, come and look at this. Isn't it rather high?'

Riordan came to her and checked the gauge, then her own notes. 'Do it again,' he said.

Some people would have found the lack of a please or thank you off-putting, but Naomi knew much better. His manners she took for granted, as she did his vast knowledge of his subject. They just worked like this as normal – with the minimum of fuss.

Something was definitely off here, and now she too was

beginning to feel it, beginning to sense what Riordan had always instinctively known.

Most volcanic eruptions followed, to some extent, a pattern or routine, this Naomi knew. There were three types of eruption: explosive, quiet or intermediary. All three could be predicted, to a certain extent, via seismic activity, geomagnetic readings, tiltmeter readings and other accurately recorded data, which together built up the picture of a volcano about to blow.

Here on Hawaii, most eruptions were of the rather oddly named 'quiet' type, meaning that the volcanoes didn't have magma highly charged with volcanic gases. Instead, they erupted by discharging a bubbling stream of lava, which could flow very fast and sometimes cover great distances before cooling.

So far, according to current theory, their own little mountain shouldn't be behaving like this. There had been none of the seismic activity usually associated with an upcoming eruption. Similarly, the tiltmeter readings, though showing some signs of swelling, were hardly enough to be alarming. But now this.

Riordan was worried, she could tell. And now she was worried too.

Bending, she began to take another reading. Then she couldn't help but smile. Well, at least this was taking her mind off her personal problems. There was nothing like standing on a volcano, which you thought might be about to blow its top at any moment, to put the rest of your life in perspective.

Take the day before yesterday, for instance. The day they played hookey, which was now fast taking on the feeling of a day that had never happened at all. Or at least had happened to somebody else in another lifetime.

After asking him, incredibly, stupidly, unthinkingly, if it was all right for him to love her, what had she expected him to say? What *could* the poor man say?

He'd been trying to let her down gently, that much was obvious now. So why oh why hadn't she seen it then? He must have realized she was reading far more into their day off than he'd meant, and had been trying to cool it off. Why hadn't she just let him, instead of making such an incredible fool of herself?

After they'd got back to the apartments, he hadn't offered to take her to dinner and by then, thank heavens, she'd at last regained enough self-respect not to suggest it either.

Yesterday, she'd been like a cat on hot bricks, wondering if he was feeling half as embarrassed as she, and scared stiff that this would put an end to their working relationship too, but he had been his usual self. They'd gone to work together, talking in the Jeep about the weather and the latest reports from the GPS system, and once in the office had interpreted data, written up reports, liaised with the HVO Seismic Network, and even worked late on the near-real-time seismic signals automatically detected and processed by CUSP, otherwise known as the California Institute of Technology's USGS Seismic Processing. It had, in fact, been very much business as usual.

Obviously, he'd been determined to forget the whole sorry episode had ever happened, and so must she.

Except that she couldn't. She just couldn't forget that he'd kissed her. Didn't *want* to.

She sighed heavily now, and lifted the temperature gauge to read it, determined to concentrate, and then quickly showed it to him. It was still high. Very high.

And then the earth moved.

Literally.

One moment she was standing beside him, both of them checking the temperature gauge, the next minute she was stumbling against him, the little rocks and pebbles skittering around her, tinkling like chime bells as they scattered and rolled down the mountainside.

Riordan dropped the meter he was holding, grabbed her as she cannoned into him, slipped and went down backwards, hard. Everything it seemed, for that scant second of shock, seemed to be moving backwards with him.

Naomi yelped, and wouldn't have been human if sheer terror hadn't seized her, as the very earth beneath her feet became something you could no longer rely on. She had that second of total disorientation that always comes with any earthquake, before realizing she was falling down, and her hands came out instinctively to save herself, scraping her skin. Her body, though, fell not on hard stone but on something much softer.

Riordan, in fact.

The earth became still. The birds, however, didn't sing. Everything became so quiet, for a moment, that she wondered if she'd gone deaf. Or died.

Then she looked down into the blue eyes beneath her and knew that she still lived.

'Now *that* registered on the Richter scale,' Riordan said, and began to laugh.

Naomi also, began to chuckle. She knew what it was, of course. A little bit of shock, coupled with relief from near unbearable tension. But the laughter was still exquisite and lovely.

'I suppose we should go and see if the tiltmeters have been

affected,' she said, well aware that her whole length was lying atop him. All the sensors in her skin seemed to burgeon to life, like rosebuds after rain.

She made no effort to move.

Riordan nodded, but his arm, which had come around her waist to hold her securely to the shelter of his body, only tightened.

'I suppose so. Or take some gas readings, see if anything was released.'

Naomi nodded. 'And take more ground temperature readings. See if the ambient temperature on the ground is localized to this side of the elevation or . . .'

Riordan kissed her.

It was a slightly clumsy, almost desperate kiss, but Naomi didn't mind. His hands in her hair were dusty and scraped from where he too had put out his hands to save her, but she didn't care about that either. His lips slewed across her face to nibble on her earlobe and she shuddered and closed her eyes.

Yes. Oh yes.

She threw her head back, letting him kiss her throat and neck and the small hollows and dents in her shoulders, revealed as he roughly pushed the material away from her.

She gasped then sighed meltingly as he became bolder. More sure. His hands moved from her back to her sides, then around, to cup her breasts through the dirty khaki material of her blouse.

She moaned.

Above her, unseen by the two lovers, a small plume of wispy smoke rose from the crater of the volcano and was quickly dispersed and scattered on the winds, just as if the volcano too had sighed.

She rolled to one side, uncaring about the little pebbles that pressed against the bare skin of her legs and lower arms. Riordan rolled with her, his hands fumbling with the buttons on her blouse until she brushed them away and quickly undid them herself, her hands snaking behind her back to unhook her bra.

Riordan sighed, very softly, as her creamy breasts came free, and then his head lowered, the chestnut highlights in his thick, wavy nut-brown hair the last thing Naomi saw before closing her eyes.

His mouth on her breasts felt hot and urgent, and her back arched as he sucked one nipple deep into his mouth. He moved his arms under her, trying to cushion her from the rocky ground, uncaring that her weight on them made the dust and rocks only grind harder into his own skin. His lips lowered, dipping into her navel, and her fingers feverishly unzipped her shorts. She wriggled out of them, sitting half upright as she did so, taking the opportunity to push her hands through the gap in his own shirt. Then she dipped her head to lick the salt from his chest, the soft hairs there like a caress against her hot face.

Her fingers ran the line of his rib cage, caressing, mapping him, like a woman reading erotic Braille, and then she was falling back again, his hands behind her head to protect it, his blue eyes blazing into hers.

Asking a question.

For answer, she reached out and unzipped his own shorts, pulling him free, loving the way his face tightened and tensed as she held him, presumably vulnerable but in reality utterly masculine, in the palm of her hand.

He moaned. Long, low, hard.

She hooked her legs around him, pulling him into her, arching her back and crying out, her voice sharp and primordial, like the cry of an eagle, as he entered her, her voice echoing and re-echoing off the mountainside.

Riordan groaned, losing all sense of self and self-control as she dug her heels into his buttocks, her young, lithe, fit, determined body dancing a rhythm against his, making him wild. He thrust, harder and harder, oblivious to everything, as she cried out his name triumphantly over and over again.

Above them the mountain sighed again, and again the small, seemingly insignificant plume of smoke was captured by an eager trade wind and dispersed. But deep in the heart of the mountain, as if roused by the heat of the lovers, the fire goddess was stirring with an answering heat of her own.

Pele was awake.

Chapter Nine

Naomi wriggled her shoulder to try and get comfortable against the hard ground, realized it was never going to happen, then sat up with a sigh and began to fumble with her clothing. Beside her, Riordan rose lightly to his feet and did the same. Small pebbles, sand and smears of dirt clung to his naked skin.

She reached up to his calf and brushed it free of debris, her fingers curling around to caress his shin bone. He paused in the act of zipping up his shorts and looked down at her.

A dry leaf was stuck in her hair, and he noticed, for the first time, her palms oozing a little blood. His eyes darkened. 'I'm sorry,' he said, thickly.

Naomi, in the act of awkwardly pulling up her shorts, glanced at him, frowning, then away again. 'I'm not,' she said firmly.

Riordan smiled gently. 'I meant,' he said, 'that I could have found us a more comfortable spot. Somewhere with grass at least.'

Naomi laughed, turning her face up to him, her blue eyes dancing. 'I don't think we had much to do with choosing the spot,' she argued teasingly. 'The earth tremor and our own hormones did that for us.'

Riordan laughed softly and nodded. 'I suppose it did,' he agreed. He felt mellow. Relaxed. Calm. At peace and at ease. And then he thought about what had just happened, and what might happen because of it, and shook his head. 'Naomi,' he said, but she quickly stood up, hooking her bra back into place as she did so, and shook her head.

'Don't,' she said softly. 'Whatever it was you were about to say, I don't think I want to hear it. Not unless you're going to tell me something nice.' She looked at him, then smiled ruefully. 'And you weren't, were you?'

Riordan reached for his shirt and shrugged it back on, his face turned resolutely away from her. But he owed her the truth, and they both knew it.

'No, I suppose I wasn't,' he agreed flatly.

Naomi tucked her blouse into her shorts, then ran a hand through her hair, dislodging the leaf from her short blonde locks.

She'd never done anything like this before in her life. Never made love out in the open, spontaneously, and without thought for consequence or propriety. Indeed, if she really thought about it, she would have said that she wasn't the type to do something like that.

Just shows what I know, she thought, fighting back the insane desire to giggle.

Riordan picked up his backpack, glancing desultorily at the instruments inside. For once, he felt no great desire to start setting up the scientific paraphernalia and listening to the secret language of the mountain. For once, something else was far more important.

Naomi glanced at him, beginning to feel nervousness edge into her happiness, eroding it like acid. His hair was mussed, and his elbows too, she noticed, were oozing a little blood where they'd been scraped in the fall.

'I've got some antiseptic and cotton wool in my pack,' she said and, searching around for a convenient boulder, sat down and began rooting through her things. By the time she'd found the necessary, he was squatting in front of her.

'You first,' he said firmly, taking it off her and dabbing some antiseptic on to a cotton wool ball. Reaching gently for her hand, he began to clean her palm. She winced, but wouldn't have traded the intimacy of the moment for any amount of discomfort.

Her body throbbed contentedly with the afterglow of love-making, and she wondered if he could possibly feel the same.

Or was it really different for men?

'Are you going to explain what you meant the other day?' Naomi heard her own voice saying, and wondered where it could be coming from. 'That crack about not being allowed to love you. What was that all about?'

But perhaps, she thought hopelessly, as his head shot up and his blue eyes pierced hers, perhaps her subconscious had got it right. Perhaps they needed to get this out of the way now, or it would be a stumbling block forever in her path whenever she tried to reach this complex and puzzling man.

She raised one eyebrow in question, determined not to get maudlin and to keep drama at bay. This was too important to let him find a way out of it.

They needed to talk. And now seemed as good a time as any.

Riordan, as if reading her mind, felt the tension drain out of his shoulders, as if defeat was some sort of medicine, and smiled wryly. 'I must have sounded like a right nut case,' he mused wryly.

This woman never ceased to amaze and impress him. She

seemed fearless, whilst he blundered about, making a mess of things.

'Just tell me,' she said softly, reading in his eyes all the thoughts which he never thought would pass his lips.

He looked at her again, wondering. Could it really be that simple? Was she really as strong as she seemed? Would this be the catharsis that would set his whole world spinning on its proper axis again, at least giving him a chance at happiness? Or, when he'd told her the truth, would she run from him, as any sane woman must?

Naomi held her breath, as scared as she'd ever been in her life, for she could feel her whole future pivoting on this one moment.

Riordan finally nodded, sank back on to the ground, leaning his back against another boulder, and looked at her levelly.

'Veronica tried to kill me,' he said flatly.

Her eyes widened in shock, and he could almost hear the mental cogs in her mind spinning as they sought for traction. 'And she tried to kill herself too. That night, the night of the car crash,' he added sadly.

Naomi let out her breath in a long and forceful sigh. Whatever she'd been expecting, it hadn't been this.

'Start from the beginning,' she said softly, reaching out with her grazed hands to take his own in hers. 'You can tell me anything,' she said, forcing his blue eyes to look into her own, making him see the truth there. 'I'll be on your side. No matter what.'

Riordan swallowed hard, looking down at the dust and dirt beneath his feet, then looked up again.

'It started off as a fairy tale,' he said hoarsely. 'Veronica was like every man's dream. Beautiful, miles above me socially, bright, bubbly and just vulnerable enough to make me feel protective and proud of the fact. She clung like a kitten, and I liked that.' He frowned, shaking his head, perhaps seeing himself as he had been then with pity and perhaps remorse. 'I suppose any man would like it,' he muttered thoughtfully, wondering if he was only trying to let himself off the hook. 'But I didn't realize just *how* vulnerable she really was. How . . . unstable.'

He looked down at their joined hands and sighed heavily. 'At first, everything was fine. I earned enough so that she didn't have to go to work, and she had a large-scale social life which kept her fully occupied. Parties. A little modelling. That sort of thing. And I rose steadily in the rare ranks of academe, at least enough to keep her proud of me, and let me think I was taking good care of her.'

Naomi didn't like the way he was beating himself up, but she wisely kept her own counsel.

'But she needed more taking care of than I could give her,' Riordan carried on, still staring at their entwined hands, too afraid to look into her eyes and read condemnation there. 'More care than any single man could give her, I guess. She became a secret drinker. I don't know how long or how far she'd sunk before I realized what was going on. I think, perhaps, a long time. She was very clever. I persuaded her to go to a clinic.'

He looked out across the pristine green forests which rose up the mountain towards them to about 6,000 feet, before the landscape became rocky. In the trees, birds sang and flowers bloomed, and overhead the sun burned down out of a tropical sky, but he was far away from here.

Naomi held her breath and simply listened.

'She hated it in the clinic,' he carried on. 'She called it a prison. Her brother visited, and I'm sure smuggled her in some booze. And worse. Yes.' He looked at her at last, hopelessness, anger and remembered frustration rife in his eyes. 'She was on drugs. Designer stuff, trendy death in a little pill.'

He shook his head and looked away again. 'I tried everything. She refused to go into another clinic, so we tried private therapists, psychiatrists, hell, even a faith healer once. Nothing worked. Then there were the men. Other men.' He swallowed hard as his voice became tight and dry. 'A lot of them.' He turned away, not daring to even accidentally catch a glimpse of her face now, sure he would see in her eyes an old, familiar look.

The same look that used to be in Veronica's eyes. The look that said, '*Just what kind of a man are you?*'

Naomi reached out and captured his chin, feeling the line of bristles in his firm jaw-line, where he would soon be in need of a shave, her fingers firm in their grasp.

Reluctantly, he turned his face to hers.

'Were you still lovers?' she asked quietly, and he laughed grimly.

'Hell, no. We were in separate bedrooms by then. In separate lives. I tried to keep her from the precipice but it was almost as if she was determined to go over,' he said bitterly. 'She was like a lemming, unable to fight the instinct to jump. But she wanted to take me with her. I can understand why,' he added grimly, but Naomi was already shaking her head in denial. 'I failed to help her, so it was my fault too. I deserved to go over the edge as well.'

'No,' Naomi said firmly. 'Riordan, listen to me. She was ill. Mentally and probably physically ill too. It's not your fault, any more than if she'd been struck down with, say, cancer.'

Riordan closed his eyes and ran his fingers over them

wearily. 'Yeah, that's what my friends said too,' he acknowledged bleakly.

'You have some smart friends.'

Riordan said nothing for a while, then, slowly, his voice husky with remembered emotion, he carried on. 'That night – the night she died. We'd been to a party – nothing wild, nothing out of the ordinary, but she'd drunk too much as usual. She wanted to drive but I wouldn't let her, and that made her angry. No, more than that, it made her furious. Her mood swings by then were just. . . .' He shrugged helplessly. 'Anyway, I got the keys off her and drove away. But she kept swearing at me, mocking me, telling me about all the men at the party that she'd slept with. And then I gave her an ultimatum. I should never have done it. Not then. Not when she was in that state.'

Naomi quickly put up a finger to his lips. 'Wait,' she said softly, urgently. 'Riordan, think. Was she ever in a *better* frame of mind? Or was she always like that by then?'

Riordan blinked, thinking back, and then stared at her, startled. Because she was right. And, for the first time in years – long, hard, hellish years – he felt the pain at last begin to leach out of him. 'You're right, of course,' he said gruffly. 'There wouldn't have been any better time. I told her that if she didn't book herself into a detox clinic that I was going to divorce her. And she went wild. I mean, really wild. She started screaming at me, lashing at me, trying to get at my face.' He ran a hand through his hair, and Naomi's heart ached at the way it trembled.

'I swerved the car and tried to push her off, but then she released the seatbelt and launched herself at me. I yelled at her that she'd kill us both, and tried to slam on the brake, but by then I think the idea had already come into her head. She could see we were on a deserted stretch of country road, with big trees either side of us. She deliberately tramped her foot down on the accelerator and yanked the wheel to point at this huge oak tree.'

Naomi closed her eyes for a moment, shuddering, seeing it all. Then her eyes snapped open, determined to be there every inch of the way for him, as he carried on hoarsely.

'But when we hit the tree, I was still wearing my belt and she wasn't,' he whispered. 'She went through the windscreen and died, in an instant, still cursing me.'

For a moment, everything was silent. Then, far down below them, a kalij pheasant called raucously to its mate, and Riordan shivered.

'So that was it,' he said flatly.

'But it wasn't, was it?' Naomi said quickly, almost aggressively, and when he looked at her, pale, spent and obviously shocked by the unexpected hardness of her voice, she took a long, shaky breath of her own.

'If that was the end of it, you wouldn't have become a monk,' she said. 'You wouldn't have built that great big wall around yourself and posted up all those "Keep Out" notices. You wouldn't still be beating yourself up over something that wasn't your fault. You wouldn't,' she said, lowering her voice, then reaching up with his hands to press them tenderly either side of her face, 'you wouldn't be afraid of me. Of either loving me, or having me love you. What did you think, Riordan?' she said quietly, firmly, looking him in the eye and daring him to deny the truth of what she was saying. 'Did you think I was going to turn into a clinging vine? Do you really think that I'm going to start pouring secret dribbles of vodka into my morning orange juice, just because you move in? Or am I going to start meeting strange men with little packets in the middle of the night, just because we become lovers? Is that it?'

He flushed. 'No! Of course not. You're nothing like Veronica!'

Naomi nodded. 'No. So what was it, then? What was the big taboo that had to keep us apart?' Her eyes searched his, then, suddenly, understood.

'Naomi, please,' he said, but it was too late.

'Oh, I get it,' she said softly, nodding her head. 'You still blame yourself for everything, don't you? It wasn't Veronica's fault she self-destructed. It was your fault for not stopping her. No woman is safe with you, is she, Riordan?' she said, her voice cracking with a heady mix of pain, pity and anger. 'Oh, you idiot!'

Riordan, far from looking insulted, clung to her hands just a little bit harder, recognizing salvation when he saw it.

'I don't need protecting from you, my darling,' Naomi said helplessly, wondering where she was ever going to get the words to explain this to him, so that he understood. What good were mere words in the face of so much devastation?

'I don't need saving from you either,' she carried on. 'I don't need you to look after me, or watch over me, or make my decisions for me, or take responsibility for my life. I can do all that for myself. I have been doing that for years. Riordan, I only need you. Us. Together. If that thought doesn't scare you too much.'

Riordan licked his lips, gone bone dry. 'I don't know,' he said helplessly. 'I just don't know.'

'Children,' Naomi carried on relentlessly, 'marriage, or a commitment, whichever you prefer. Old age together. Do any of these things appeal to you?'

Riordan closed his eyes. Did they appeal? He almost laughed. The thought of making love to her again, holding her

153

again. Having laughter and life in his universe again. Did it appeal?

'Does light after darkness sound good?' he asked at last, wondering if she understood. If she could ever understand.

And then he looked at her. He dared, at last, to look at her with nakedness in his eyes, and found that yes, miraculously, she did understand.

'I love you,' she said simply. 'Kiss me.'

And so he did.

Jago Marsh said goodbye to his mother and waited impatiently as the telephone receiver was put down, then picked up again a few moments later.

'Hello, bro,' Keith's cheerful voice came blithely over the line, and Jago tensed, staring unseeingly out of the window at a ferry boat cruising out of the harbour, probably on its way to Maui or Molokai.

'I want to know the truth,' he said flatly, his voice as cold as an arctic winter. 'About Charis Scott and what happened between you. I want to know what really happened last summer, and in detail. And Keith,' he said ominously, 'if you know what's good for you, no more lies.'

Even thousands of miles away, Keith Marsh shivered at the menace in his brother's voice. He sat down, hard, on the nearest chair and decided that perhaps it was just as well that this showdown should come when they had half the world between them.

'It wasn't true,' he said, his voice an apologetic whisper, feeling the old familiar guilt wash over him. 'Everything was the other way round.'

Jago swallowed hard, hooked the phone line over his arm, walked to the terrace chair, sat down heavily, closed his eyes, opened them and leaned back.

'Tell me,' he said flatly.

So Keith did. All about the very married Californian beauty, sparing himself nothing.

'All right,' Jago said, when he'd finally finished. 'I can understand how that happened. You were young and stupid and she was beautiful with a heart of stone.' Perhaps some of it was even his fault? He'd probably been over-protective of the boy, shielding him from life's knocks when he should have been warning what living was really all about.

He probably, Jago thought with a pang of guilt, hadn't done his brother any favours at all.

'So, chalk it up to life and move on,' he said, deliberately unforgiving. 'Now, tell me how any of this involved Charis Scott.'

There was a long silence as, back in England, Keith Marsh prepared to get his head ripped off.

'I needed a cover story,' he said at last, taking a deep breath. 'Her husband was the jealous type, and she had a pre-nup which meant she'd get peanuts if he divorced her for infidelity. So she insisted that we were discreet, and that I was seen to be interested in someone else. And that someone was Charis. I mean, I'd met her, and we hit if off. I liked her,' he rushed on, before his brother could explode. 'So we went out a few times, but then she found out I was seeing this other woman, and that she was a married one at that. And Charis is really a conservative type, you know,' Keith gabbled on, as Jago closed his eyes again and swore at himself, over and over again. 'It's the way she was brought up, I guess.' Keith unknowingly continued to hammer nails in his brother's coffin. 'She's a stand-up lady. Anyway, she told me off, and I mean she really gave me a piece of her mind, and told me never to darken her doors again. And, of course, when the love of my life found out, she was furious, and dumped me,' Keith said, managing to sound, at last, ironic. 'So I came home,' he finished.

And waited. He didn't know it, but he'd finally grown up in the last five minutes.

Jago took a long, hard breath. 'When I get home, I'm going to skin you,' he said quietly, and hung up.

He sat for a long time, his hands dangling loosely between his knees, going over every moment he'd spent with Charis Scott, seeing all the signs he'd missed. Seeing all the mistakes he'd made. Seeing all the misunderstandings in the cold, hard light of reality.

She'd been badly used by his brother, and instead of apologies and peace offerings, he'd come to Hawaii to teach her a lesson which, by rights, she should have been teaching *him*.

He'd mauled her when he should have been handling her like the precious jewel she was. He'd been planning to take from her her most prized possession, when really he should have been offering her his.

No wonder she hated his guts.

He laughed, a harsh, grim, darkly amused laugh.

'So this is what it's like to get your comeuppance,' he mused out loud.

He didn't like it much.

But he could take his lumps.

What worried him more was putting things right. But how? A mere apology for his brutish behaviour was hardly going to cut the mustard. She'd throw any gesture back in his face – and who could blame her. Not himself, for one. In fact, as he pictured her in his mind's eye, throwing his bouquet of roses back at him, or emptying his peace-offering bottle of champagne all over his head, he found himself grinning.

Charis was a spitfire. A conservative, old-fashioned gal who'd have his guts for garters if he didn't come up with something worthy of her.

And there was only one thing, of course.

He had to get back her *Heart of Fire*. And prove he hadn't stolen it.

And tell her he loved her.

Whatever she thought that might be worth.

Jago laughed again. Was that humility he could feel, coming a-calling on him like a stranger in the night.

He didn't like that much either.

He reached for the phone again, lifting it on to his lap, and began dialling Kal's number. Perhaps the offer of a reward – a very, *very* substantial reward – might help. Not that any collector would care about mere money, or be willing to part with a new, prized acquisition because of it. But someone else must know who had the statue. The thief who stole it, for a start. And it was amazing how a fortune could loosen even the most tight-lipped of mouths.

And to get back Charis Scott's respect, Jago was prepared to lose far more than just a fortune.

'So this is love,' Jago said wryly.

He'd get used to it.

The next day, Riordan pulled into a rare parking space at the university and made his way to the head of science's office. The report he had to turn in needed to go right to the top.

He'd left Naomi back at the lab liaising with the head of the Volcano Hazards Program of the US Geological Survey. There was also a geophysics expert in that morning that he wanted her to talk to. It was time to start ringing the alarm bells because something was telling him that by the time he waited for confirmatory data to start coming in, it might be too late.

Way too late.

Instinct told him that Kulahaleha was going to erupt soon. Perhaps too soon for any of them to be ready for it. And whilst he was sure he still had enough anomalous readings to at least make others sit up and take notice, he was enough of a realist to know that it was up to him to stick his neck out, if he wanted to get things done.

If he was wrong, it would be a major setback to his career and reputation. But he couldn't bet lives on that.

He was in luck. The dean was also in the head of science's office, and when his secretary buzzed him in, Dr Jim Akuna introduced the head of the university. 'I think you may have already met?' he added, as the two men shook hands.

Riordan nodded, took the seat offered, and, as the dean made sounds to leave, asked him to stay.

'Jim, this isn't just a social call,' he said quietly to the head of science. 'I want you to look at this.'

Dr Akuna's field was astrophysics, but Riordan had been careful to explain his data so clearly a layman could under-stand it. He saw the physicist's face drain of colour as he read quickly. The dean quickly lost his affable administrator's look and became distinctly sharp-eyed.

'You have the figures for the latest seismographic event,' Dr Akuna said, and Riordan nodded. 'Page three, near the bottom. And another thing. We observed smoke from the crater this morning. It's still building.'

The dean leaned slowly forward in his chair. 'Are you telling us that you think Kulahaleha is going to blow?' he asked, obviously surprised.

Like most islanders, he was used to living with volcanoes,

and if he wasn't exactly blasé about it, he was not inclined to panic easily. Besides, in his experience, when a serious eruption was due, practically everyone and his auntie knew about it. The signs were obvious, sometimes for weeks prior to the event.

'It's not following the usual set patterns,' Riordan said flatly, as if reading his mind, 'but the tiltmeter readings don't lie. The magma chamber is flooding.'

'But that doesn't always signify an eruption, does it?' the dean asked cautiously.

'No,' Riordan agreed. 'Sometimes it drains off.'

'The earthquakes don't look that severe,' Dr Akuna put in, a little tentatively, realizing that this was hardly his area of expertise, and very much aware that he was talking to a man who was considered top in this subject.

'No. But they're strange. Their epicentre is anomalous,' Riordan said firmly. 'I've seen this happen only once before, I admit, in Iceland. But it was disastrous. Nobody was prepared for it. Many people died.'

Riordan took a deep breath, and looked the head of science in the eye. It became, suddenly, very quiet in that room. 'In my opinion, we'll have a major eruption in the next two to three days. Maybe even sooner.'

Rudy walked cheerfully into the university's main hall and looked around. Spotting a giant wall chart, he ran his eyes down it until he found the room number assigned to Dr R.J. Vane.

Unlike his vast lab space and office room back at the observatory, Rudy was childishly delighted to find that the university itself had allocated the illustrious Dr Vane a mere cubby-hole of an office, situated on the second floor, next to a rather smelly chemistry lab.

The door, not surprisingly, wasn't locked. He walked in, careful to shut the door behind him, and looked around, grimacing at the dust on the venetian blinds in the one small window, and the rows of boring technical journals lining one wall. A grey, depressing filing cabinet was locked, and he supposed that that was where Riordan kept his files, such as they related to his university business.

Rudy had found out that his brother-in-law was obliged to give one tutorial lecture a month as a condition of his two-year appointment to the observatory, and Rudy pitied his poor students.

Who would want to listen to his brother-in-law for two solid hours?

In fact, Dr Vane's lectures were widely attended, even by non-volcanologists, as his reputation preceded him wherever he went, and he was known to be an eloquent and passionate speaker.

Rudy walked to the desk, sat down in the swivel chair and desultorily opened the drawers. He glanced uninterestedly at the stationery, then at his watch.

Ten minutes to go before Harris McVie was due to meet with the dean.

Rudy hadn't found it hard to learn the details of Harris McVie's itinerary, for it was part of his job to be 'available' to people, especially men who called up his secretary claiming to represent a local firm interested in sponsoring a couple of students in an engineering scholarship.

No doubt the dean of the university was courting Harris McVie with an eye to his own funding as well. Which fitted in with Rudy's plans very nicely indeed.

With a smile that would have made the Cheshire cat envious, Rudy opened the big shopping bag he was carrying and looked inside.

He winked down at the object inside.

'Don't worry, sweetheart,' he said cheerfully. 'You won't have to stay in the dark for much longer.'

Riordan left the building feeling alternately relieved and worried. He knew that Dr Akuna and the dean would, even now, be calling on the civic authorities to give them news of his report. The fire departments, police, emergency services, perhaps even the national guard, would all be alerted.

And if it was for nothing then his name would be mud.

But at least the people immediately living around the volcano would be warned. And at the first sign of trouble, people would be prepared. Even if it only meant grabbing the cat and gunning the Jeep to head for the coast.

He missed Harris McVie by about two minutes, so when the funding chairman walked into the dean's office, it was to find an unexpectedly frantic hotbed of activity.

Dr Akuna hastily explained what was going on, and apologized for the dean, who was on the phone to the mayor.

Harris McVie listened, his big red face showing very little sign of emotion, until Dr Akuna was finished.

'So, Dr Vane thinks there'll be an eruption,' he said thoughtfully. 'Tell me, do his colleagues agree?'

Dr Akuna looked at him in some surprise, wondering if he was just imagining it, or was there a certain edge in the bluff American's voice?

'So far, they're not inclined to jump one way or the other,' Dr Akuna said cautiously. 'Dr Vane was very up front about that. But they agree that the readings are anomalous, and that the volcano is definitely active. And Dr Vane has something of a reputation for calling eruptions accurately. Enough for us to take him very seriously indeed. Why?' he asked bluntly.

And, on the telephone, the dean listened with half an ear to the mayor's private secretary giving him the runaround, and the very interesting conversation going on between the head of science and his other visitor.

'Oh, nothing,' Harris McVie said casually. He knew too much about the fragility of a man's reputation, especially in the world of academe, to be loose with his lips. 'Dr Vane is one of four short-listed people which our finance committee is considering for a sizeable grant, that's all.'

Dr Akuna nodded, immediately satisfied. He understood only too well the constant grind to find funding, and about the caution of those who handed the funding out.

'So Dr Vane is considered sound then?' Harris said, conversationally.

Dr Akuna nodded. 'Oh yes. Very.'

'Well, I can see you're busy. I'll reschedule another appointment with the dean's secretary,' Harris said, showing himself out.

Once outside, he paused thoughtfully. So, the rumours about Dr Vane's drinking and mental health certainly hadn't got this far. Which was strange. Usually, whenever an academic was in trouble, the university was always the first place to know.

As he approached the secretary, he paused for a moment, giving in to a rare moment of spontaneity, but considering, under the circumstances, that it was justified. Dr Vane had just committed himself to predicting an eruption. So he must be sure, even if others weren't. And Dr Akuna for one seemed to have faith in his judgement. So, if the eruption happened, he, Harris McVie would recommend to his committee that Dr Vane be awarded the grant. If not, then the funding would go elsewhere. He already knew several people who'd expressed an interest in donating to the butterfly conservation scheme, so it shouldn't present any problem for his conscience, either way.

This decision made, he nodded to himself, made the new appointment with the secretary, then walked out into the outer hall. He was just passing the wide sweep of steps leading to the upper floors when he heard a noise.

'Psst!'

Startled, he looked up, spotted the man from the bar leaning over the railings, and narrowed his eyes as the man beckoned dramatically for him to come up the steps.

Harris, naturally intrigued, did so, meeting Rudy on the landing.

'I need your help,' Rudy said at once, looking madly worried, and all but dragging him along the corridor and into a deserted, rather dreary office.

'You're someone important, aren't you?' Rudy said, looking anxiously at the American. 'I mean, around here,' he said, waving a hand to encompass the entire university.

'Well, I'm not on the faculty, you understand,' Harris began cautiously, wondering if he might have made a mistake. This man was acting almost demented. 'Look, what is all this about?' he demanded, beginning to get annoyed. This was the second time this strange man had all but waylaid him.

'It's about my brother-in-law,' Harris hissed. 'Dr Vane, you remember? I'm scared he's really gone over the top this time. I was waiting for him in his office here and look what I found.'

Rudy pointed dramatically to the desk.

And on the desk was a statue.

It was a statue of a woman, emerging from a volcano.

Chapter Ten

Harris McVie stared at the statue for a few seconds, wondering why it looked familiar, and wondering even more why it should arouse such angst in the near-stranger beside him.

Then he remembered several things, all at once. First and foremost, an incident at the party of the Princess Charis Mina Scott, a week or so ago. Harris now easily recalled how the old man in the wheelchair, the grandfather, had been talking about the statue, which had been in his family for generations, and about the legends attached to it.

Harris and several others interested in mythology, archaeology or ancient artefacts had gone to the library with the old man, and had been proudly shown the treasure. In the event, it had been well worth the lecture, for the object had been a striking, half-finished piece of breathtaking power and primitive artistry.

And looked exactly like the object now on Dr Riordan Vane's desk. But how on earth had it got there?

Slowly, and feeling a growing sense of reluctance building up at the back of his mind, he walked to the desk, Rudy trotting eagerly beside him, for once not talking. He was finding the American's reactions far too satisfactory not to just sit back and enjoy.

Harris reached out and touched the statue gingerly, as if it might disappear at the first sensation of human interference. The rock felt warm to the touch, as if fired by its own inner heat.

'You know what it is, don't you?' Rudy said at last, letting awe creep into his voice. 'It's famous. And worth a fortune.'

Harris nodded. 'Yes. It's the *Heart of Fire*. Unless it's a copy. Or a fake.'

Rudy sighed. 'I don't think there were any fakes made. Why should there be?' he asked, oh so reasonably. 'Crooks would know that collectors would be only too well aware that there was only one original, and that it was in Hawaii. Nobody would bother to fake it, because nobody would ever be able to sell it.'

Harris nodded, having already made the same mental argument himself. It made perfect sense.

But now he was remembering something else. 'A few days ago,' he said softly, 'I was approached by a young man who said he was a reporter. He wanted to ask me about the party Princess Charis Scott held at her home. He said he wanted to get an inside scoop on a typical island high-society party. I didn't believe him.'

Rudy looked at him closely, and a little impatiently, wanting only to get on with his own scenario, but sensing the big American wasn't merely talking to hear the sound of his own voice, and for once displaying some patience.

'No?' he prompted.

'No,' Harris said. 'For several reasons. The first being that I know a lot of reporters, and I know how they operate. And this man didn't fit the bill. Secondly, he asked some very odd questions. For a supposed gossip columnist he wasn't very interested in who was chatting up who, or what lady was wearing the biggest baubles. He was far more interested in this statue. Although trying, very carefully, not to appear interested in it at all.'

Rudy nodded, uninterested, but quick to see a way to turn it to his advantage. 'Could be. Or it might have been a private enquiry agent, working for the Scott family. If the statue was stolen (and it obviously was, because I can't see why they should have lent it to Riordan), then they'd obviously take steps to get it back.'

'Why not just call in the police?' Harris asked, although he was, to a certain extent, simply playing devil's advocate here because he had a sneaking suspicion that his companion was right. For, the very next day after talking to the supposed reporter, Harris had been talking to a real journalist, one covering a local story at the hotel where he himself was staying, and he'd happened to see his inquisitor again.

Harris wasn't all that surprised by the coincidence of it all. It was a small island, after all, and there were only so many places for people to go. And Harris's hotel was a popular spot with many people, especially locals.

So he'd simply thanked his good luck and pointed out the stranger to his reporter friend, asking if the other worked at his paper also. He hadn't been particularly surprised when his journalist friend had taken one look, laughed, and said that Kal Ahuna was about as much a reporter as his Aunt Fanny.

Naturally, Harris had been intrigued and was soon listening to the Kal Ahuna story, the real 'Magnum PI' of the Big Island.

At the time, Harris had simply mentally filed it under 'curious' and shrugged it all off. With the blissful certainty that he'd done nothing personally to warrant the attentions of a private eye (he wasn't even married, so no wife was seeking divorce evidence), and guessing, even then, that the PI had to be working on something to do with the wealthy and famous Scott family, or one of the guests at the Scott party, he'd merely dismissed the whole episode.

But now, here was the same coincidence cropping up all over again.

Or was it?

Harris looked from the statue to the man beside him. 'I'm sorry, I've forgotten your name,' he said politely, and Rudy smiled ingratiatingly.

'No reason you should remember it, old chap,' he said, and thrust out his hand again. 'Rudy Carter.'

'Right. And you're Dr Vane's brother-in-law, that right?'

Rudy nodded. 'Right again. As I said just now, I thought I'd catch up with old Riordan and take him out to lunch. Fellow does nothing but work and sleep, and not so much of the latter, if you ask me. That's one of his problems, I reckon. Insomnia. Either that, or he's gone right off his rocker. I mean . . . look at it!' he said, pointing helplessly at the statue again. 'What the hell am I going to do? I don't want to see him get into trouble but we can't leave it here, can we?'

Harris, much to Rudy's surprise, didn't immediately agree. And if he'd been a mind reader, he'd have been even more disconcerted. For Harris was nobody's fool, and he was think-ing hard.

Why had this man singled him out at the bar the other day? Now that he thought about it, he'd done nothing but talk about his brother-in-law then, dropping ill-concealed hints about his secret alcoholism and fragile state of mind.

Why would a stranger do that? And could it possibly be a

coincidence that he should pick on himself, Harris McVie, who had a vested interest in Dr Riordan Vane?

Harris didn't think so.

Add to that, the fact that he himself hadn't seen any signs to worry him in Dr Vane's manner, and the volcanologist's own colleagues obviously had extreme faith in him, certainly enough to take his predictions of an eruption seriously, and what did it add up to?

Something fishy. Most definitely fishy. And now this.

Harris, like most intelligent men, didn't appreciate being taken for a ride, or used as anybody's patsy.

Harris looked around the office thoughtfully. If he knew academics – and he did – he would bet his bottom dollar that Dr Vane spent as little time here as possible. Just enough to conscientiously fulfil his obligations to the university and his students, but nothing more.

So would Rudy Carter seriously expect to catch him here? And again, why had he chosen the exact same time when he himself had an appointment here?

Just what was this character up to? And what, exactly, did he want of him? For Harris McVie had no doubts now that he was supposed to be playing some sort of role in Rudy Carter's own private drama.

'Well, what do we do?' Rudy said, an edge to his voice now. 'Call the police, or what?'

Harris slowly shook his head, watching Rudy's face closely, and not missing the brief look of anger and frustration which blazed across the back of his eyes.

'Oh no, I'm sure the university wouldn't want that,' Harris said slowly and carefully. He was very much aware that he'd walked into a minefield, and wasn't about to step on anything explosive if he could help it. He had his own neck to worry about, after all.

'I think the best thing we can do is contact this private detective I was telling you about, and tell him about the statue. I guess he must have some sort of an interest in all this. If we hand it over to him, he can contact the Scott family and arrange for its return.'

Rudy opened his mouth, then closed it again. A cunning look came into his eye. 'I suppose that would be best,' he agreed slowly.

Harris glanced at the statue again, wondering exactly what in the hell was going on. And, all too human-like, wondered if he shouldn't just walk away from this whole situation and wash his hands of it. You never knew when messing around in someone else's business was going to backfire on you. Especially when it involved the wealthy and the powerful, such as people like the Scotts.

'Why don't you put it back where you found it?' Harris said. 'In case Dr Vane comes back?' Then, he added mentally, let's get out of here.

Rudy nodded and walked obediently around the desk, lifting the statue down and carefully laying it on its side in the big bottom double-drawer. He shut it carefully, and looked up, sighing heavily.

'What do you think the Scotts will do? Will they prosecute him?' he asked, for all his woebegone expression, an avid tone tingeing his voice with spiteful glee.

Harris shrugged. He was now convinced more than ever that this man had his own private agenda, and almost certainly wanted him to say that, yes, he was sure the Scotts would prosecute. And, again human-like, he felt the urge to puncture his balloon.

Besides, he rather liked Dr Riordan Vane, and didn't partic-

170

ularly want to see him get into trouble.

'I'm not sure,' he said at last, dampeningly. But he imagined that it would be the case. He couldn't see Princess Mina Scott or her grandfather letting someone get away with stealing their property.

He turned and walked to the door, glancing back over his shoulder at the entrance way, catching a look of malevolent glee on the man's face as he did so.

Rudy quickly turned on a brave little smile. 'Oh well, I suppose it's for the best. At least Riordan will get the help he needs now.'

Sickened, sure that, whatever this man wanted to happen to Dr Vane, it had nothing to do with his best interests, Harris left.

Rudy waited for a few seconds then reached down and extracted the statue. He put it back into the shopping bag he'd been carrying, walked to the door, cautiously checked that the coast was clear, and walked out.

As he skipped lightly down the stairs, he was vaguely aware of a sense of dissatisfaction. Things, for some reason, hadn't quite gone as he'd planned.

By rights, Harris McVie should have been shocked, maybe angry, but certainly self-righteously determined to do the right thing. So why hadn't the annoying little man hot-footed it to the first telephone to call the police, as Rudy had expected? What was all this about calling in a private detective and letting Charis Scott and her family do the dirty work?

And then he realized, and smiled cynically. Of course – he should have known. The man didn't want to get dragged, even as a mere witness, into a criminal case. This way he kept right out of it. Really, Rudy should have expected it. Self-interest was something he would always understand.

As he emerged into the sunshine, Rudy even began to smile. Perhaps it would work out even better this way? Riordan would be arrested, disgraced and ruined. The prominent Scott family would see to that.

Especially when he played out his final hand.

Rudy laughed.

It was a real humdinger of a hand. A veritable royal flush. There would be no way that even Riordan Vane would be able to talk his way out of the mess it would put him in.

It would be the final cherry on top of the cake which would be Riordan Vane's ignominious downfall. He only hoped that his Vee, wherever she was, was looking on and chortling too.

Kal had not long put down the receiver on Jago Marsh, his ears still ringing with the Englishman's impatience and demands for positive action, when the phone rang again.

He picked it up, frowning down into his computer terminal, as a vaguely familiar American voice drawled deeply into his ear.

'Hi, is that Mr Ahuna. Mr Kal Ahuna?'

'Yes.'

'This is Harris McVie. You might remember me. You were passing yourself off as a gossip columnist the last time we met.'

Kal abruptly straightened in his chair, recalling the man and the face, and feeling extremely discomfited to be found out in a lie. For a man who told a lot of lies, Kal was usually very adept at never being caught out in them.

'Er, yes, Mr McVie,' he said cautiously. 'What can I do for you?' His eyes fell to his private investigator's licence, a copy of which he had hanging on his wall. His eyes were rather anxious.

Over the line came a deep chuckle. 'Relax, Mr Ahuna. I'm ringing with information which I think you might find interesting. And you don't even have to pay for it. All I need is your assurances that my name will be kept out of things.'

Kal frowned. 'Exactly what things are we talking about, Mr McVie?' he asked cagily.

Harris coughed. 'Let us say, I believe that something went missing from a certain house at a certain party. And that a certain man had been hired to find that certain something. Would you think me very over-imaginative?'

Kal sat up even straighter. 'I can't say as I would, Mr McVie, no,' he said craftily.

'So if I told you that I had seen that missing object, not ten minutes ago, in the office of a certain eminent volcanologist, who was also at the party, you wouldn't consider it all that unlikely?'

Harris was rather enjoying himself. Spy novels, in particular those of the master, le Carré, were always his favourite reading. And who knows when he'd ever get the chance to make a phone call like this one again? Never in his lifetime, he suspected. So he could, perhaps, be forgiven for making the most of it.

'Thank you, Mr McVie,' Kal said softly.

In his telephone kiosk, Harris smiled, almost regretful to be hanging up so soon. 'You're welcome, Mr Ahuna. Oh, and before you do anything else, I think I should warn you that there's something going on – something other than the obvious, that is. If I were you, I'd make enquiries regarding a certain Mr Rudy Carter. I rather think he has an agenda of his own.'

And with that very satisfying exit line, Harris McVie hung up.

Jago opened the door on only the second ring, surprised to see his visitor. 'Hello, Kal, come on in.' He wondered if the PI was the sensitive type and had come to tell him he'd quit. But he didn't think so. For one thing, the detective was grinning hugely, and for another, Jago hadn't put him down as the wilting flower type who'd back off after his first rollicking.

'I've found it,' Kal said, coming straight to the point. 'Or rather, to be more accurate, I've had a tip-off as to its whereabouts from a very reliable and respectable source. A man who was also at the party that night.'

'Who?' Jago said sharply, but Kal shook his head. 'He wants to remain anonymous and I agreed. But he told me that he'd seen the statue not more than an hour ago. And I must say, I was rather surprised by what he told me, although it all fits. In a way. The man who took it was at the party, and might be said to have an interest in the statue, albeit a rather weird one.'

Jago walked to the bar, poured out two fruit juices with ice and walked back, handing one over.

'So who took it?' he said flatly.

'Dr Riordan Vane. He's a volcanologist over here on the island for two years, working up at the observatory.'

Jago paused in the act of lifting the glass to his lips, wondering why the name sounded familiar. But once he'd cast his mind back to the party, he quickly came up with the answer.

'I met him there,' he said flatly. 'We talked briefly. He didn't look the thieving type to me,' he added, his eyes hardening on the PI. 'And I'm usually a good judge of character.'

'I don't doubt it,' Kal said, meeting his eye without flinching. 'And I don't mind admitting Dr Vane wasn't on my serious suspect list either. But my source has nothing to gain by saying he'd seen the statue where he had, and has no private axe to grind. I checked that out before I came over here. However, he did mention someone else who seems to have an interest in the statue, but I haven't had a chance to check him out yet. But I will.'

Jago grunted, absently swirling the ice cubes in his glass, his lean, hard face intent on some thought or emotion the PI couldn't have interpreted had he been offered a million dollars.

Then Jago looked up. 'I want it in writing. A full report, starting with when I hired you, what you did, or had done, and ending about this latest tip-off.'

Kal looked surprised. 'You want it all? But you know what I've been doing.'

Jago Marsh smiled wryly. 'It's not for me. I want someone else to read it, so dot all the Is and cross all the Ts. You've got an hour.' Then he smiled and indicated his PC. 'You can use that. I'll attach the printer,' he added magnanimously.

Charis looked up from her architect's latest figures on what would be needed to keep Kokio Aloalo Palace sound for another century or so, and gave a huge sigh. The cost was exorbitant, but worth every penny.

She swung her chair around, glancing out of the window just in time to spot her grandfather's wheelchair disappear behind some pilo bushes out in the garden.

She smiled tenderly. He was probably going to check up on the gardener and make sure he'd watered the pukiawe shrubs in the big border. He had a particular fondness for those.

175

She walked to the windows, watching the blackburn butter-flies and lava crickets on the kilauea naupaka flowers, and absently reached out through the open pane of glass to pluck a blossom from the a'ali'i, which grew tight against the wall. This bright scarlet bloom she tucked absently behind her ear.

She envied her grandfather his love of the garden. At least it gave him something to do, even if the gardeners all regularly threatened to quit if he kept interfering. But of course, they didn't mean it.

Time was hanging heavily on her hands now she no longer had an office to go to.

She looked up as the butler knocked discreetly on her study door and came partway inside.

'Mr Marsh, to see you, your royal highness.'

Charis's lips twisted bitterly. For one moment she longed to say 'chuck him out' but didn't, for various reasons.

One, she couldn't really ask her rather elderly and totally proper butler to do something so demeaning. For another, it would create gossip within the household, which was bound to get back to her grandfather, and he had enough worries already, without wondering if his granddaughter had gone out of her mind. And, besides all that, she was curious as to what he wanted.

'Show him in, please,' she murmured, knowing, even as she spoke, that she couldn't have said anything else, even if her life depended on it.

Because she wanted to see him. If only for a few moments. If only to fight, shout, be hurt, or hurt back. She was beginning to feel addicted, hopelessly and helplessly, to the sound of his voice, the glare of those steel-like eyes, the sight of that taut, scarred face.

She sat down quickly, all but falling into her chair, understanding at last that she was in love.

She hadn't thought it was supposed to be like this.

'Mr Marsh, your royal highness,' the butler intoned, and Charis looked up blankly.

She was in love. With this man. What was she going to do? Jago walked in, a flat green folder in his hand, his eyes immediately pinning her to her chair like a butterfly to a specimen board.

She was wearing baggy scarlet culottes, and a jade green, red, yellow and azure top. In her long dark locks a red flower gleamed. Her exotic beauty was so unforced, so much a part of her, that he wondered how he had ever doubted it was real.

He walked to the desk, sat down unasked, and pushed the folder towards her.

'I want you to read that,' he said simply.

Charis blinked. Business? He wanted to talk *business*? Now? At a time like *this*?

Then, with a diving heart which hit her shoes like a lead weight, she realized that there was no 'time like this' as far as Jago was concerned. Why should there be? Just because she'd been stupid enough to fall head over heels for a cold-hearted iceberg of a man didn't mean that he felt a pile of beans for her.

It was a hard lesson to learn but Charis supposed she'd better get used to them. Feminine instinct warned her that there were many harsh lessons which this man could teach her.

Wonderful ones, too, if only . . .

Grimly cutting off her thoughts before they got her in even deeper water, she reached for the folder and opened it up, surprised by the first report. She glanced at the heading, vaguely recognized one of the top PI firms on the island, and began to read.

After the first sentence, she was hooked.

She read every page, from the dry reports of Kal's operatives who'd questioned the valet parking attendants on duty the night of her party, to his sometimes comical conversations with an Australian kleptomaniac lady, to his final entry.

The sighting of the *Heart of Fire*.

Her own heart leapt. It was not lost. It was still on the island!

She slowly closed the folder and looked at him.

'It could be a trick,' she said at last. 'You could have paid this man, this Ahuna, to fake all of this. Your hiring him. Everything.'

Jago nodded. 'I could have,' he said impassively, 'but I didn't. And do you really think, if I had stolen the statue, that I'd go to all this trouble?'

Charis laughed grimly. He had her there. Boy, did he ever. 'No,' she said miserably. 'I don't suppose you would. My feelings hardly count, do they? If you had the statue, you'd be long gone by now.' There was, after all, nothing keeping him here.

Jago stared at her. 'You might sound a little more grateful,' he said at last. 'The statue is practically back in your hands again. Isn't that worth anything to you?'

Charis blinked. 'What do you want?' she said angrily. 'A medal? Do you want me to pay the PI's bill? Is that why you came here?'

Jago stood up. His eyes glittered like diamonds. He leaned slowly forward, planting his fists widely on her desk, bringing his head level to hers.

'No, it isn't,' he growled. 'I wanted to get you back the statue. I wanted you to realize that I hadn't taken it. I wanted an apology.'

'When snowballs freeze in hell!' she snarled instantly. This was better. She knew where she was with this old familiar antagonism. At least it distracted her from contemplating the new, desolate wasteland that had just taken up residence where her heart used to be.

'And I wanted to give you an apology as well. About Keith,' he carried on, as if she hadn't even spoken. 'I had it out with him, and he told me all about it. He used you shamefully, and I'm sorry. And he will be too, you have my word on that,' he added grimly.

Charis, flabbergasted, waved a hand vaguely in the air. Why wasn't he playing the game? Why wasn't he shouting back at her? And what, exactly, was she supposed to do with this new, kinder Jago Marsh?

'Oh, that doesn't matter. I haven't given Keith a thought since I gave him a piece of my mind,' she said helplessly.

Jago smiled. 'So, the statue's as good as recovered,' he said softly.

Charis glanced down at the green folder. 'Yes,' she agreed, but in truth, her mind was far from the recovery of the statue.

She looked at him again. 'Thank you,' she said flatly.

Jago frowned. 'I thought you'd be happy,' he said, puzzled.

'Oh, I am,' Charis said, trying to put some enthusiasm into her voice. But it wasn't easy. When you'd just had the wind taken out of your sails so comprehensively, when you were suddenly presented with the man you loved, in the full knowledge that he was only vaguely aware that you even existed, it was hard to take anything else that life had to throw at you with any appearance of vim or vigour.

Jago shook his head, laughing softly at himself and slowly straightening up. He thrust his hands into his pockets and sighed tiredly. 'OK, I give up,' he said wearily. 'What do I have to do to earn your forgiveness?'

Charis blinked, looking up at him blankly. 'Forgiveness for what?'

Jago looked down at her, his eyes searching her face, her lovely, heart-shaped, doe-eyed, beloved face.

'For the way I've been treating you, of course,' he said. 'You can't say that you and I have been kind to one another.'

Charis smiled ruefully. 'No,' she agreed. They hadn't been kind. 'But there's nothing to forgive in that. Oh, all right, if it means so much to you,' she added, as he opened his mouth, obviously about to argue the point, 'I forgive you. There. Satisfied?'

'Hardly,' Jago said sardonically. He slowly sank back into his chair and stared across at her. He couldn't remember feeling quite this helpless before in all his life.

He'd thought recovering the *Heart of Fire* for her would, if not put it all right between them, at least go a long way towards it.

Instead, she seemed hardly interested. In fact, she seemed to find even talking to him a chore.

He felt a shaft of fear lance through him as the awful thought that it might all be too late washed over him. That he might not, after all, be able to win her over. That he might have lost her. Just because he wanted and loved her didn't mean he could make her feel the same way about him.

For a man who'd never considered failure before in his life, such thoughts didn't sit well.

'All right, Charis, take what you want. I don't mind. Whatever it is – a pound of flesh, humble pie, hell, even a demand that I beg. But don't push your luck too much on the last one. Whatever you want, just tell me. It's yours.'

Charis stared at him, utterly lost. She shook her head.

Jago leaned forward again on the desk but not in an attitude of challenge this time. Instead, the look on his face was as close to appeal as she instinctively knew he would ever come.

'What do I have to do to have a chance with you?' Jago explained patiently. 'Come on, woman, you must know you've won.'

Won? Won what?

Charis again shook her head, and his eyes became bleak. 'You don't want me at any price then,' he said, his voice harsh and cracked. 'I can't say as I blame you. But don't think I'll give up because I won't,' he flashed. 'I know that you felt something too, that day, in my apartment. Don't try and pretend you didn't.'

He got up and walked around the desk, pushing her chair easily away from the table, and leaning over her. His finger lightly brushed the flower in her hair. Her eyes, when she looked up at him, were enormous.

'W-what exactly are you trying to say?' she asked breathlessly, because suddenly, bubbling up like a hot spring through rock, a sense of happiness was beginning to permeate her entire being. He seemed to be saying something wonderful. Wasn't he?

Jago's finger moved from the flower in her hair to the side of her cheek. He seemed fascinated by the soft downy texture of her skin. 'Hmm?' he said softly, then met her eyes again. Puzzled. Hopeful. Dancing.

'I'm trying to say that I love you,' he said, forcing the words out with some difficulty. 'That I want you,' which came easier. 'That I'm crazy about you,' which wasn't hard at all. 'That, from the moment we met, you've been getting under my skin,' which was nothing more than the truth, 'haunting my dreams at night and . . . umph!'

Charis, launching herself upwards and into his arms, knocked him off-balance, pushing him sprawling backwards across the desk.

Papers scattered as his arms came out to save himself, but she was already crawling on top of him, her small hands hard against his chest, pushing him down on to the wood.

'You'd better not be up to something,' Charis said warningly, smiling down into his stunned eyes. 'If you're playing games with me, I'm telling you . . .'

She swooped down on him, her lips hot and hard against his, demanding and insistent. For a moment he stiffened, shock and surprise hardly letting him believe what must be happening to him. Then his arms came around her, pulling her closer, his legs splaying slightly, allowing her to put one bent knee between them.

Charis ran her hands feverishly between his shirt buttons, popping off two in her haste to get them undone. His chest, covered with fine wheat-coloured hair, was already bronzing to the colour of pale toast, from his time under the hot island sun.

She pulled the shirt from the waist band of his slacks, bending her head to dip her tongue into his navel. He jerked beneath her as she did so, his feet kicking her chair spasmodically, sending it skittering back into the wall.

'Charis,' he groaned, looking down as she all but ripped the shirt off him, utterly excited by her passion, impressed and already responding to her wildness, even as a warning voice at the back of his head told him to make sure.

He knew that she was not the kind of woman to take lovemaking lightly. That, in all likelihood, she might regret this in the morning; and that thought was enough to make him feel like crying.

'Wait a minute,' he husked, striving desperately to keep it light. 'Do you make a habit of throwing your male guests on to your desk and ravishing them?'

Charis lifted her head from his navel, contemplated him for a moment, liking the high flush of colour staining his cheekbones and the raw, naked, helpless look of passion, which turned his eyes to molten steel, and shook her head.

'No,' she told him. 'But for you, I'll make an exception.'

She knew why he'd stopped her, of course, and loved him all the more for it. He wanted to give her a chance to change her mind. To take a breath and think about what she was doing.

But for once, Charis didn't give a fig for appearances, or consequences or anything else. Now that she had Jago Marsh just where she wanted him, she wasn't about to let him go.

She licked the length of his lower rib, loving the way it made him gasp and squirm, but then his hands were around her waist, lifting, turning, overwhelming her, and suddenly she was underneath, and his lips were lowering on to hers.

He kissed her face, her ears, her neck, working lower, kissing her skin through her blouse, fastening on the hardening nub of flesh on her breast as she groaned helplessly.

He pulled her top up over her head, her glorious black hair splaying around her and cascading over the edge of the desk. He looked down at her naked breasts with a tenderness mixed with greed, which made her want to crow about it from the rooftops.

Then his lips were on her exposed flesh, and she arched her back, raking her nails down his spine, hungrily seeking a way to bare skin.

Jago paused to yank off his shirt, ripping it slightly, and tossing it uncaringly on to the floor like so much rejected flotsam. Her nails, painted bright scarlet, clawed his shoulder, raising tiny love-weals on his back as he sucked one rosy nipple hard into his mouth.

She fumbled with his belt, managing to get it open, raising her head from the desk as he sat back on his heels, his face as tense as a high wire, the white scar on his face standing out in stark contrast to the high, passionate spots of colour on his cheeks.

He peeled off her culottes, running his hands lovingly along her calves as he did so, making the heat pool at the centre between her legs, and her eyes darken to the colour of the black volcanic rock which was so prevalent on the island.

He pulled down his own slacks, moving back over her, his hands either side of her head, his own wheat-coloured hair hanging down off his forehead, making her reach up to push it back.

'Charis,' he said again, but she was once again reaching up to him, pulling him down to her, her legs parting to pull him urgently inside her, her mouth opening sweetly as a long, urgent, hungry sigh feathered past her lips.

Jago made an echoing sound, its perfect mate, moving smoothly inside her, feeling the feminine molten heat surrounding him, pulling him deeper inside, caressive, demanding, and undeniable.

His flanks tightened with raw masculine power, but he was careful, gentle, thoughtful, until she bit his shoulder and screamed his name.

Then they were dancing impetuously, unstoppably, to the same tune, a hot, undulating tune which caught them up, riding on ever higher waves of passion and near-pain, desire and unselfishness, until finally depositing them on a far, satiated shore.

Chapter Eleven

Jago looked across at her as he turned the Jeep on to Volcano Road. 'You OK?' he asked softly.

Charis stretched, smiling like a sleepy cat. 'I'm fine. Don't worry about me,' she said.

'I *do* worry about you. I like it,' Jago added, almost surprised himself by the simple truth of his words. Charis, sensing it, looked at him, raising one eyebrow in gentle query.

Jago shrugged, overtook a stalled Jeep, and gunned the motor again. 'I'm not used to being in love, I suppose,' he said defensively. 'I always thought it was something to be avoided. No, not even that. I always thought it was a myth. At best, something which happened to other people, not to me. I suppose that's why I felt so antagonistic towards you, right from the start. I suppose, on some deep level, I knew you were dangerous.'

Charis laughed happily. 'Is this true confessions time?' she asked, but her voice was indulgent, and underneath, serious. She knew what it must be costing this proud man to say such things, and she wasn't insensible to the honour he was doing her.

Her body still tingled from their love-making, and she

straightened her top a little self-consciously as they headed past the Kilauea Visitor's Centre, and the host of tourists scattered around it.

'In that case,' she carried on, letting her hand rest briefly against his on the steering wheel, 'I have to admit that I was fascinated by you even before we met. And when we did, you bowled me over.'

Jago laughed. 'I don't think so,' he drawled.

'Oh, but you did,' Charis insisted. 'I was just determined that you'd never know it.'

Jago glanced at her, his heart in his eyes, turning them from steel to dove-grey. 'You did a good job.'

He glanced back at the road, which was winding upwards steeply now, towards the observatory, and pulled to the side of the road. He couldn't say what he wanted to say and drive at the same time.

He turned sideways in his seat, the better to look at her. Just half an hour ago they'd been making love. He already wanted her again. Firmly he pushed such thoughts aside. 'We need to talk,' he began cautiously, and Charis felt her heart leap.

Already today her world had been torn apart and reassembled. First she'd been in despair, thinking she'd fallen a victim to unrequited love. Then he'd come into her office and made love to her, and as if he meant it. From despair to desire in nought-point zero seconds.

From a normal, dull life to one fraught with possibilities. Already she was reeling. Now, she knew, there was more to come. She tried not to be scared as she too turned in her seat, and studied his face. What if it was bad?

He looked serious. His scar, standing out more and more as he became tanned, seemed to beckon her to touch it. To run

186

her fingertips over that symbol of pain and make it go away. Then she shook the thought off. If ever a man didn't need pity, or protecting, it was Jago Marsh! As she should know!

'This sounds ominous,' she said lightly, determined not to become a clinging vine. What if he said he only wanted a casual affair? Or began one of those awful 'no commitments' speech men were so fond of. She was not about to let either of them down. Her own pride wouldn't let her show him how vulnerable she was, and she would die before she'd do anything to embarrass him.

Jago forced a smile. 'It does sound kind of ominous, doesn't it,' he admitted. 'But I'm a straightforward kind of man. I like things simple. Honest and out in the open.'

Charis nodded, feeling her heart pound. Here it came. The polite brush-off.

'I want us to get married,' Jago said.

Charis gulped.

'I know what you're going to say,' he added, rushing on before she could speak. 'We've only known each other a few weeks. And for most of those, we were at loggerheads. And I'm not saying we can't or shouldn't have a long engagement. But I want to make it clear. To you, my family, and the rest of the world. We're together.'

Charis gulped again.

'I'll talk to your grandfather, of course,' Jago continued firmly, 'and once we've got the statue back, and got that whole mess sorted out, I don't see why he would have any objections. Obviously, I'm not titled, but I do have money and position.' Jago paused, then looked at her, almost humbly. 'You know him better than I do. Will it be a problem?' he asked.

Charis took a breath. 'Haven't you forgotten something?' she asked mildly.

Jago's heart fell, then rallied. 'What?' he barked belligerently. Whatever dragon she was about to thrust forward, he'd slay it. Nobody was going to keep them apart. Nobody and nothing.

'You haven't asked me,' she said meekly.

Jago blinked at her. 'What do you mean?' he asked, genuinely baffled.

Charis grinned. She couldn't help it. She'd been so prepared for the worst, that now she could afford to be a little cheeky.

'I mean,' she explained patiently, 'that you're assuming *I* want to marry *you*. What if I don't? What if I see you as a summer fling? Or even a part-time lover?' she asked, curious to see what he'd say.

Jago stared at her. 'Don't be daft,' he said. 'You're not the kind to bed-hop. And do you really think I don't know when someone loves me back?'

Charis put her hands on her hips – not easy to do when sat in the passenger seat of a Jeep – and gawped at him. 'Well, I don't see why you should be so sure,' she said warningly. 'After all, you didn't know you were in love with me until just now.'

'Oh yeah,' Jago said, beginning to enjoy himself hugely. 'And just when did you know you loved *me*?' he challenged.

Charis's face fell. Then she too began to grin. 'OK, you got me there,' she admitted.

'So the answer's yes?' he said.

'The answer's yes,' she agreed demurely.

'And your grandfather won't mind?'

'Of course not. He only wants me to be happy. And you'd better make me happy, or else.'

'And there's no sort of taboo or anything?' Jago asked warily. 'No ritual or family thing forbidding you to marry anyone but your second cousin on your royal side or some such thing?'

Charis gurgled. 'There'd better not be.'

'So where do we live?' Jago asked. 'Here or England? My business is in England.'

'My home's here,' Charis pointed out firmly. 'I'm an island girl, through and through. Can you see this' – she pointed to the flower blossom in her raven locks – 'going down well in Surrey?'

Jago leaned back in his seat. 'Berkshire, actually,' he corrected her mildly. 'I live in Windsor.'

'Near the castle?' she asked, excitement creeping into her voice.

Jago grinned. 'Why can't we live six months in England, six months in Hawaii?'

Charis considered it. 'I don't see why not. I might quite like to see snow at winter. Or maybe not.'

'We'll be married here,' he mused thoughtfully.

'Oh yes.'

'Children?'

'Six?'

Jago paled. 'Three,' he compromised desperately.

Charis cocked her head. 'Chicken,' she said softly, and leaned across to kiss him.

'Anything else?' Jago asked, eyes gleaming, as she pulled her lovely face away from his.

'Keith?' she said tentatively.

'Keith is going to be fine about it,' Jago said. 'We'll forgive him, and he'll grovel for the rest of his life. Sound fair?'

Charis grinned. 'Fair. Will your mother like me?' she asked anxiously.

'Mum will love you. She's been desperate for grandchildren for years. And she's beginning to worry that I'm becoming a confirmed bachelor. Believe me, she'll fall on your neck. Besides, her son will be marrying a princess. What mother could ask for more?'

Charis gave him a vicious dig in his ribs with her elbow.

'So,' he said, on a sigh, absently rubbing his ribs.

'So,' Charis agreed. 'Isn't it supposed to be harder than this?' she asked then. 'I mean, for other couples. It's not supposed to be this simple, is it?'

Jago considered her question seriously. 'We're not like other couples,' he said cautiously.

Charis laughed joyously. 'Quite right,' she agreed complacently. 'I love you.'

'I love you too.'

'Good. You better had,' she warned, then waved her hands ahead of her. 'Well, go on. Drive. We've got to have it out with Dr Vane. Find out why he took my statue.'

'Our statue,' Jago growled gruffly.

And for one instant she felt a shaft of alarm. Surely he wouldn't be marrying her just to get his hands on the *Heart of Fire*?

She shot him a quick look. He was surreptitiously looking at her out of the corner of his eye, a small line of merriment tugging at his lips.

And Charis felt her heart swell with happiness. 'Oh, I'm going to make you so miserable,' she said warningly.

Jago turned on the engine. 'Whatever you say, sweetheart,' he said softly.

Rudy Carter parked his Jeep beside a piece of scrub, looking up at the volcano with thoughtful eyes. It was smoking. Definitely. From the top of the crater, white wisps of ash drifted across the azure sky.

So this was Kulahaleha. Looked like a big hunk of rock to him.

He walked forward, making out the trail which visitors, walkers and scientists alike had all made up the western side of the mountain, and looked around nervously. Good. So far, no sign of Riordan and his assistant.

He knew that, within the hour, a small tour of academics was due to inspect one of the stations. He'd noticed the poster about it on the university's bulletin board, stating that Dr Vane would be giving a talk in situ. Which was just the sort of audience he needed.

He carefully took the statue from his bag, hardly even aware of its beauty, as he searched for the perfect spot. It had to be where none of the visitors could miss it. And there, off to his left, right beside the small sheep-like trail which rose and twirled around the mountain, was the perfect place. A piece of rock, flat-topped, almost like a table.

He put the statue carefully down, but as rock met rock, he felt a small frisson of fear creep up his spine. For a second there it had felt as if the base of the statue had become magnetized, as if another force other than his own had pulled the *Heart of Fire* on to its natural pedestal. He experienced a moment of deep atavistic superstition, as if he'd just been a witness to something primeval.

Then he angrily shrugged the feeling off. It was nothing. He was imagining things.

He turned and, sweating profusely now, began to climb further up the trail to where he knew Riordan and his blonde assistant were carrying out some tests.

He wanted to be there when the fun started.

He wiped his face with a handkerchief, feeling his heart straining. Damn, it was hot today. The heat even seemed to be coming up through his shoes. Which was ridiculous, of course. Heat came from the sun, not the ground.

Behind him, tiny pebbles cascaded down the mountainside as a small earth tremor shook the ground. It was so minor that Rudy didn't even feel it, except as a weird vibration which seemed to lodge in his chest.

He turned and looked back.

The statue of Pele regarded the mountain top thoughtfully. The plumes of ash were getting thicker. On its pedestal, the statue vibrated a little as the earth shook again.

But the statue did not fall.

'I'm sorry, sir, madam, but Dr Vane isn't in his office. He and his assistant are on Mount Kulahaleha. But, wait, you can't go there,' the young man from the observatory said urgently, as Jago and Charis turned to leave. 'Dr Vane has issued an imminent eruption warning. We've posted them up already in those settlements around the volcano, and it's gone out on the internet. And as of now, all tourist spots in that vicinity are closed, and the mountain itself off limits. We've even had to cancel a group of visiting academics from the university who were due to go up there this morning.'

Charis swallowed hard. 'You say the volcano is going to erupt? But we haven't heard anything about it.'

'No. It's unusual,' the grad student admitted. 'But Dr Vane is sure. Or at least, sure enough to call in the civil authorities. Can I leave him a message and have him get back to you?' he offered, trying to be helpful, even though he was obviously very busy.

Jago looked at Charis, a question in his eyes. Charis shook her head.

'It's all right,' Jago said urbanely. 'We'll try and catch him later.'

They walked back into the car park, aware now of the activity which seemed to be going on all around them, turning the usual staid and quiet observatory into an ant's hill of industry.

Jago opened the door for her, watched her settle her shapely legs under the dash, then reached for the seatbelt and handed it to her. He watched her buckle up then shut the door and returned to the driver's seat.

'What say we head on down to Punaluu?' Jago asked breezily. 'Get some sun and sand and sea?' He wanted to see her in a bikini. Maybe even find a quiet little spot under a coconut tree . . .

'Let's head back to Hilo,' Charis said firmly.

Jago sighed. 'Yes, ma'am.'

But when they got to the turning to her house, she shook her head. 'No, carry on. Into town.'

'Don't tell me you want to go shopping,' he groaned.

But Charis didn't want to go shopping. A while later, she pointed. 'Turn there. On to Saddle Road,' she said.

Jago turned on to the rather rough road which cut across the island, more or less bisecting it in the middle, from east to west, joining Hilo to the Kona-Kohala Coast. Most people took the coastal road and after a few miles Jago could see why. This one began to climb and lurch in ever-increasing hostility, as the majestic peak of Mauna Kea rose to their right, with the shorter peak of Kulahaleha in front of it.

Already he noticed some police cars were busy setting up detour signs, and one car pulled across in front of them as they approached.

He looked across at Charis swiftly as the police waved them to a stop. She was already smiling sweetly.

Which had to mean trouble.

'*Aloha*,' she called gaily, as one of the men recognized her and, touchingly, saluted. 'We're just off to Waimea,' she said, before they could even ask. 'There's not a problem, is there?'

'No, ma'am, so long as you don't stop,' the other officer replied, and explained about the precautions being taken.

Charis looked suitably worried, and promised them that she'd make Jago put his foot down. Jago rolled his eyes and faithfully promised to obey. Once they'd pulled ahead, however, and the police cars were out of sight, he looked across at her knowingly.

'We're going up the mountain, aren't we?' he said grimly.

Charis nodded. 'We are.'

'By that, of course, you mean that nothing's going to stop you from going, and since I won't let you go alone, that means we both go. Right?' he clarified.

Charis nodded, eyes flashing. 'Isn't it nice that we know each other so well? And already?'

Jago laughed ruefully. Yes. Wasn't it?

But he'd never been so happy in his life, so what the hell?

Rudy heard them talking long before he saw them, and crouched down behind some scrub. Cautiously, careful to avoid tripping over the rocks, and cursing the ever-growing heat, which seemed to be bouncing off the land and creating a very un-Hawaiian-like sauna of the air, he manoeuvred himself into position.

A hundred yards or so ahead, he could see Riordan and the blonde woman, bent down by some equipment, conversing rapidly. Occasionally the wind brought a few snatched words his way – 'ambient ground temperature,' and a comment about a tiltmeter, whatever the hell that was. It all sounded very urgent. So perhaps he wasn't imagining the heat coming from the ground after all?

At last, Rudy began to feel fear. He was standing on a volcano, after all. One which was spewing smoke, and seemed to be hotting up.

But nothing was going to make him leave now. Soon the academics would arrive and see the statue. One or more might even recognize it. Certainly, they'd demand to know what it was doing there. And then what would the good doctor say?

Obviously, he'd deny all knowledge of it, but he had Harris McVie to back up his claim that it had been in his office. And by now, Charis Scott or that useless grandfather of hers may even have called in the police.

And not for anything in the world would Rudy Carter miss the opportunity of seeing Riordan Vane carted off in handcuffs.

Jago stalled the Jeep and, sighing, parked it at a precarious angle, making ultra-sure of the handbrake.

'Well, this is as far as we can get by road,' he said, looking across at her. 'Feel like walking? Those shoes don't look too sturdy to me.'

'Stop trying to talk me out of it,' Charis grumbled, climbing out of the Jeep and looking around. But she was secretly pleased. It was a new sensation, to be looked after so assiduously. She rather liked it.

Once outside the air-conditioned Jeep, the heat struck her almost at once. Used to the islands, the trade winds, and the vagaries of the summer months which could sometimes throw up strange weather patterns, Charis nevertheless felt deeply uneasy.

This heat was unlike anything she'd felt before.

She glanced at Jago to see if he'd noticed it, then realized that, even if he had, he wouldn't know that it was unusual.

She glanced up at the volcano, and the sight of white smoke puffing from it sent shivers up her spine. Like all islanders, she knew that you respected volcanoes. She'd lived with them all her life. She knew a lot of the scientific community who studied them; knew that tourists even travelled from all over the globe to witness eruptions. But there had been no rumours on the unofficial grapevine that this particular volcano was going to blow, and that in itself was unusual. Mostly, people had plenty of warning, sometimes weeks in advance, before a spectacular eruption.

But this wasn't following the usual pattern. Even she, no expert, could sense that. It worried her.

'Looks calm enough,' Jago said, looking up at the mountain. Although smoke and ash came from the crater, it reminded him more of a smoking chimney, or perhaps the stack of a steam engine or steam liner, rather than of anything dangerous.

In spite of that, he really didn't want to be here. Not with Charis. If he'd been on his own, he wouldn't have minded at all. But the thought of her being in danger, even a very slight one, upset him.

'Come on, let's go back,' he said. 'Dr Vane has to come back to his office some time. We'll camp out in the car park if you like. Don't worry, we'll get the statue back.'

'It's not just that,' Charis said, walking around to join him on his side of the Jeep. 'Don't you feel it?'

Jago looked at her warily. 'Feel what?'

Charis shook her head. It was so hard to put into words. 'Something's wrong.'

Jago looked around. The birds were singing. Down below, in the tree line, rainbow shower trees bloomed in profusion. But the area above them looked sparse and dark with black volcanic rock. Even with the blue sky above them, the area they were in now could be described as bleak.

'Don't you think it odd that the statue should be stolen, just when an eminent volcanologist says that a volcano which shouldn't be about to erupt is?' she asked, rather ungrammatically.

Jago ran a hand through his wheat-coloured hair. 'I'm not sure,' he said at last. All this sort of thing was new to him, but he respected Charis's instincts. As she'd said, she was an island girl. She knew these things.

'Come on,' Charis said, holding out her hand firmly. 'Now that we're here we might as well talk to him. Look, that's the only trail up the mountain, so we must be able to find him if we stick to it.'

Jago sighed heavily. 'Is there no talking sense to you?'

Charis looked at him, feeling a twinge of guilt sluice over her. 'You can go back if you want,' she said, her voice uncertain. 'I mean, I have to go on. The *Heart of Fire* was entrusted to my family. It's my duty. But not yours. It really might be dangerous, and . . .'

Jago reached out his hand.

Without another word, she took it. Together they began to climb up the mountain.

Rudy glanced at his watch, frowning. Where the hell were they? The tour had been due to start an hour ago. Don't say some feeble-mind grad student at the observatory had got them all lost.

In front of him, Riordan Vane glanced at the latest temperature readings. Beside him, Naomi did the same. And gasped.

Riordan looked at her, his eyes hard. 'Pack up,' he said

crisply. 'It's time we got off this mountain.'

Wordlessly, Naomi obeyed him.

Hundreds of feet below, Charis and Jago stared at the statue. They'd just turned the corner of the sheep trail, and spotted two Jeeps. So obviously the scientists were here. Then, a little further on, Charis had seen something standing on a rock. Another rock, or so she'd thought at first, except that something about it had seemed to call to her, even from so far away. And long before human eye could confirm it, Charis already knew what it was.

Now she and Jago stared at the magnificent statue, dumbstruck.

'It's just stood here,' Jago said at last, looking around helplessly, 'in the middle of nowhere. Anyone could steal it. Or it could fall. What's the man thinking of?'

Charis stared at the beautiful, terrible face of the fire goddess, and took a long, unsteady gulp of air. 'Doesn't it look to you as if she was meant to be here?' Charis whispered.

Jago's head swivelled as he looked at her. 'What do you mean?'

Charis shrugged helplessly. 'Just look at her. On that rock. It's as if the rock had been placed there, just for her. And above her – the mountain. The smoke. Can't you feel as if she was supposed to be here? Perhaps Dr Vane knew. Perhaps he didn't take her to sell her, or because he coveted her. Perhaps he took her because he knew she was needed.'

Jago opened his mouth, then closed it again. He understood and respected the almost spiritual connection which obviously existed between the woman he loved and the family treasure stood before them. But the man he'd met at the party that night had struck him as someone with both feet planted firmly on the ground. A man of science. A man who liked facts and figures and mechanical equipment. Not the sort to believe in ancient myths at all, in fact.

Although he was beginning to sense what Charis meant. Looking at the statue, he too felt as if it belonged.

'Well, Dr Vane can't be far away,' Jago said, forcing himself to be practical.

He didn't like the way the birds were no longer singing. Or the growing heat. And his feet kept tingling, as if something in the ground was quivering. But he knew Charis wouldn't turn back, so the only thing to do was push on.

'Let's find him and ask him what's going on,' he said firmly. Then they could get off this big piece of rock.

He walked towards the statue, Charis beside him, but when he reached out to it, she quickly grabbed his arm.

'No, don't,' she said urgently. 'Leave her here.'

Jago drew his arm back slowly. 'You sure?' he said softly.

Charis looked around her, and shivered. 'Yes,' she said firmly. 'I'm sure.'

Chapter Twelve

Jago wiped the sweat from his forehead with the sleeve of his shirt, pausing as he did so to catch his breath. 'It's so damn hot,' he said irritably.

Charis agreed. Although she was faring a little better, being more used to heat than someone from cool and temperate Britain, she too was beginning to wilt.

'We should have brought some bottles of water,' she said.

Jago shrugged. 'Too late now. And is it me, or is it getting harder to breathe?'

Charis looked down, way down, and plumbed her memory for school geography lessons. 'Are we really high enough for the air to be getting thin?' she asked. Or was it just the heat making breathing seem such a chore? 'How high up do you have to be?'

Jago smiled ruefully. 'Blowed if I know,' he said cheerfully. 'When we meet our light-fingered doctor friend, we'll have to ask him.'

They stumbled on, the climb getting harder. Once, Jago heard some shuffling in some scrub, just off the trail, and he wondered what small animal was scurrying for cover.

And if it knew something they didn't.

Rudy, crouched so low his face was almost in the dirt, watched the two people walk by, his mind working furiously. Charis Scott. What was she doing here? She couldn't be one of the academics he was expecting, unless she'd been invited along as some sort of PR thing. And wasn't the tall blond man with her that scarred freak from her party?

How come they were here?

Rudy didn't like surprises which were not of his own making, and once they'd passed, he crept further on, desperate to overhear what they were saying.

By now, Charis and Jago had also spotted the two silently working volcanologists, and Charis watched them with some surprise. They seemed to be working very fast, packing away stacks and stacks of scientific-looking gear into cases and haversacks. They weren't speaking, and something about the way they hurried made both of them uneasy.

Charis shot Jago a quick look.

Jago shrugged back, then cleared his throat. Loudly.

Naomi and Riordan both spun around, Naomi looking stunned to find two strangers on the mountain when, by rights, it should now have been cut off to all tourists.

Riordan too looked at them grimly. His glance went from the stunning dark-haired petite woman to the taller man. A brief frown played with his dark brows as a vague sense of recognition swept over him. He began walking towards them quickly.

'This mountain is off limits,' he began gruffly, alarm and surprise making him sound belligerent. 'Aren't there any road blocks up on Saddle Road yet?'

'They're just putting them up now, Dr Vane,' Jago assured him calmly, sensing the other man's angst, and feeling unnerved by it. Instinctively, and in the way men have sometimes of weighing up one another accurately and instantly, Jago was sure that panic wasn't something the other man was used to.

And, unless he was reading all the signs wrong, and he didn't think he was, Riordan Vane was as close to panic as he was ever likely to come. He looked pale, and he was sweating profusely, but it was the dark, foreboding look in the scientist's eyes which made Jago curse himself for letting Charis ever set foot on this mountain.

'We've met, haven't we?' Riordan said briefly. Then, more urgently, 'Look, you really must start back. This volcano is becoming extremely active. You have to start back now. Please, hurry.'

Rudy, taking advantage of all eyes being on the two newcomers, crept further forward. His heart began to pound in anticipation. At last, Vane was going to pay for what he did to his sister.

Naomi, keeping one ear on the conversation as she hastily continued packing, felt the ground vibrate again beneath her feet.

'Riordan, we're getting tremors,' she said sharply. 'They're almost constant now.'

Charis held hard onto Jago's hand, her fingers squeezing his tightly. 'Dr Vane, did you steal the *Heart of Fire* from my house on the night of the party?' she asked straightforwardly.

Even though an impatient voice was yelling in the back of her mind that this was hardly the time or the place, another voice, an unafraid, grimly determined voice, told her that they needed to know the truth.

And know it now.

Riordan stared at her blankly. 'What?' he said, equally blankly.

Naomi abandoned the equipment and strode quickly forward. Her eyes flashed across to the other woman, noting her beauty first, and then, after a longer, more considered look into her dark eyes, seeing her determination. And lack of criticism. Which sat oddly with her accusatory words.

When she'd first heard the stranger ask such an outlandish question, every instinct in her had screamed to come to Riordan's side, ready to do battle. Now, something else checked her.

'I'm sorry, have we met?' Naomi asked bluntly.

Charis looked at the tall blonde woman, her face streaked with dust and sweat, and saw a look in her blue eyes which she instantly understood. She glanced at Riordan, and wondered briefly if he knew how much he was loved. Being a man, probably not.

'I'm Charis Scott,' she introduced herself quietly. 'On the night of my grandfather's birthday party, the statue called *Heart of Fire*, was stolen. You've probably heard of it?'

Riordan glanced at Naomi, baffled. 'It's a statue depicting the fire goddess Pele, isn't it?' he said, and Naomi nodded in confirmation.

'Why do you think Dr Vane took it?' Naomi asked, turning back once more to Charis, her chin out, her fists clenched.

Charis shook her head. It was more to reassure the other woman that she wasn't out to damage her man than in answer to her question.

Blue eyes met black, and as the air around them boiled, Naomi Bridges and Charis Scott came together in perfect understanding.

'I'm not saying that he did,' Charis said softly. 'Or, perhaps, I'm saying that if he did, he might have had his reasons. This mountain, for instance.'

Naomi, obviously puzzled, glanced at Riordan, who was looking from Jago to Naomi to Charis and back to Jago again.

Answering the look in the volcanologist's eye, Jago said quietly, 'I hired a private detective to find the statue. We've been trying to keep it from getting into the papers, and the police have been very discreet. It's probably why you haven't heard anything about it.'

Rudy, tensed and quivering in his hiding place, listened. Half of him felt elated – at last, Riordan was being challenged. Being seen as a thief, or at best, as someone with guilty secrets. But half of him also felt deeply uneasy. Why weren't the police here? And why didn't Charis Scott and her Sir Galahad sound more angry, more accusing?

They were talking like old friends over Sunday brunch, for pity's sake. What was wrong with them?

'He telephoned me this morning, to tell me that the statue had been found,' Jago continued. 'In your office,' he added flatly.

Riordan stared at him, his jaw going slack. 'In *my* office?' he repeated at last, utterly stunned. He sounded so genuinely surprised that Charis didn't for a moment doubt him.

Besides, if someone like the blonde amazon standing beside Riordan Vane had such total belief in the man, she was inclined to believe in him herself, too.

Jago's eyes narrowed. 'It was seen in your office at the university,' he agreed, less willing to take the man at his word than Charis, but nevertheless, like her, inclined to give the man the benefit of the doubt.

'At the university?' Riordan echoed. 'But I'm hardly ever there. What's it doing there?'

'It isn't there now,' Charis said softly. 'It's back down the mountain.' She vaguely pointed in the direction behind her.

'On a rock. Did you put it there?'

Now Riordan began to frown. He looked at Charis closely. She seemed to believe what she was saying. But wasn't the statue worth hundreds of thousands? Nobody in their right mind would just leave it lying around on the mountain. Was it possible she was having some sort of mental breakdown? Or was this some kind of stunt?

But there was the man beside her. He glanced at Jago, demanding confirmation, and Jago nodded briefly. 'It's there, all right,' he said softly. 'Just stood there, right out in the open.'

Naomi shook her head. 'We didn't put it there,' she said simply. 'We'd have no reason to. And I was with Riordan at the party all night long. He certainly didn't steal it.' It was said emphatically but with no attempt to persuade. It was just a simple fact.

And Charis nodded, accepting it as such.

But she was puzzled. 'So who did?'

Riordan was still having trouble putting all this into perspective. Behind him, the smoke and ash coming from the crater began to thicken, unnoticed, belching out, gaining height and power.

'Wait a minute,' he said, holding out his hand. 'You say the statue was stolen the night of your party. It was seen first in my office at the university and now you say it's here.'

'Right,' Jago confirmed.

'Who saw it in my office? This detective you hired? Why didn't he return it to you?' Riordan persisted.

'It wasn't him who saw it,' Jago said slowly. 'He had a tip-off from a well-respected source. Both he and another man, a Rudy Carter, saw it there and—' He broke off abruptly as Riordan paled.

'Carter,' he said flatly. 'I might have known. He's behind all this, I can guarantee it,' Riordan said, for the first time since Charis and Jago had arrived, sounding angry.

Behind the bushes, now only yards away, Rudy ground his teeth. This wasn't how it was supposed to happen, dammit. It wasn't fair. Why did things never go his way? Why did Vane always seem to lead a charmed life, when he was a killer?

'Who's this Rudy character?' Jago said sharply, sensing they'd come to the crux of the matter at last.

Naomi looked quickly at Jago, then at Charis. 'Rudy Carter is the brother of Riordan's late wife, Veronica Voight Carter. He blames Riordan for her death, although it's not true. He's been making trouble for Riordan for a long time,' she said grimly. For Riordan had long since told her all about Rudy's vendetta, and his obsession with his sister. 'He even followed us here, determined to cause trouble,' she added angrily. 'The man's mad.'

Jago shifted uneasily, not sure if he'd just lost his balance, or whether the earth really had just heaved under his feet just then. From the way Charis's fingers were digging into his arm, he felt certain she'd stumbled too.

'Look, we've got to get off this mountain,' Riordan said, knowing for a fact that they'd just experienced a minor earthquake, and dragging his mind back, at last, to the immediate danger. 'I'll answer any questions you want at the police station or anywhere else for that matter,' he offered generously. 'But it'll have to be tomorrow. I'll take a lie detector test if needs be, but now's not the time to discuss this. We have to go. Now. Naomi, grab the bags. I'll get the cases.'

Jago went forward to take one of the silver-sided cases, which was heavy but not bulky, and grabbed one of the haversacks from Naomi, who smiled a vague thanks at him, her face tight and worried.

'You don't have to go to the police,' Charis said. 'I'd rather they weren't involved anyway.'

Rudy grabbed the scratchy trunk of the bush in front of him and twisted it hard, making his palms bleed. Not go to the police? Why not? He wanted Vane in jail. Jail, jail, *jail*. He wanted him to rot, for years and years and years. He bit back a sob of frustration and yanked on the bush harder, making the blood trickle across his wrists.

'We've got the statue back and that's the main thing,' Charis went on, blithely unaware of the human time bomb ticking away unseen in the bushes. 'And, besides, I believe you,' she added, almost as an afterthought.

Then she glanced up at the mountain. And her heart stalled.

Her throat went dry and she had to swallow hard, twice, before she could even speak. And then all she could manage was to point her finger and say 'Look' in little more than a strangled whisper.

Jago heard her and turned, twisting his head up and around to where she was pointing.

And swore softly.

'Dr Vane, is it supposed to be doing that?' he asked, fighting back the urge to laugh at the absurdity of what he'd just said. For the volcano was pouring out smoke and ash now as if there was no tomorrow. It was funnelling it up, higher and higher into the sky, like a mushroom cloud from a nuclear bomb, but without the death-bringing explosion.

Rudy, all but tearing the bush out by it's roots now shook his head. What did the stupid woman mean? She *believed* him. How *could* she believe that Riordan hadn't taken the damned statue? Hadn't she seen it with her own eyes, damn her? What did he have to do to get her mad? To hear her old man go on about it, the *Heart of Fire* was the greatest thing since sliced bread. How could she just shrug and say, "Oh ,I believe you" when the damn statue was stood in plain sight for anyone to see? What the hell else would it be doing on the mountain if he hadn't take it?

Why did women always believe Dr Riordan Vane? Simpering over him. Even Vee had loved him. Vee! And he not even worthy to shine her boots.

He reared up, his eyes wild, his ugly face contorted with hate.

Everyone was looking up at the mountain, their backs to him. Even now, they were ignoring him. It was always the same. Rudy didn't matter.

He surged forward, snarling, incoherent. It was too much. All that planning, all that clever, clever plotting, and still Riordan Vane came up smelling of roses.

He was so intent on his rage that he didn't even notice what the other four were staring at, as if transfixed, human statues turned to stone by the site of the gargoyle.

Or, in this case, by the sight of Pele's power.

Charis felt her breath, which had been trapped and aching in her lungs, slowly seep out of her. Where was the explosion? The geysers of fire? Why was it so eerily calm and silent?

Why wasn't she more afraid?

Beside her, Jago too was staring at the sight, his face also expressing awe at the beauty of the thing, rather than fear.

Perhaps they'd all gone mad.

Naomi and Riordan were the first to break free of the magical but potential deadly spell of the mountain. Riordan turned, caught movement out of the corner of his eye and spun around, just as Rudy Carter reached out and grabbed Naomi.

Naomi shrieked in surprise, then choked, as a hard arm slipped across her throat, bruising her neck and cutting off her air supply.

'You *bastard!*' Rudy screeched, his wide, mad eyes fixed on Riordan, who took a quick step towards him. 'Keep back,' Rudy screeched, his voice high-pitched, almost girlish. 'Or I'll snap her neck, I swear I will.'

Paralyzed by the threat, Riordan froze.

Naomi, hardly aware yet of what was happening, fought for self-control. If only she could breathe! She tried to drag in a breath, managing to get a little air into her lungs, but very much aware of the effort it was costing her. Little pin-pricks of black already spotted her vision and she tried to blink them away. Her spine, where it was bent backwards at an awkward angle, was a blaze of aching muscle. Her legs were beginning to feel weak.

Riordan looked at her, his blue eyes blazing. He'd never felt so helpless before in his life. At that moment, he could have killed the man who was threatening her life so recklessly.

Naomi tried to smile, to reassure him. Obviously it was Rudy Carter behind her, and obviously he was out of his mind. But was he really dangerous? Naomi tried to see if he had a weapon of some kind – a knife perhaps, but couldn't feel anything metallic against her skin.

She couldn't bear to see the look of helpless fear on Riordan's face. To make matters worse, she could almost hear his thoughts. He'd already been responsible for one woman's death, was he now going to have to watch her die too?

That, more than anything else, made Naomi furious. She would *not* just stand by whilst another member of the Carter clan took a stab at destroying the man she loved.

She'd be damned if she would!

Charis became aware that she was standing behind Jago. Somewhere during the last few crazy seconds, he must have reached out and dragged her protectively behind him.

Now Jago glanced at Riordan, ready to take his cue from the other man. If he wanted to rush him, Jago would be only too glad to help. There were two of them and only one of the attacker. But the blonde girl was going red in the face and obviously on the verge of blacking out. What if the maniac who'd seemed to spring from nowhere really did break her neck?

Riordan took a careful breath. 'Rudy, let her go,' he said, his voice wavering a little as he fought to stay calm. 'It's not Naomi you want to hurt, now, is it?' he tried, cajolingly, stepping a bare inch closer. If he could just get in striking range . . .

'Why not?' Rudy screeched, a little bit of spittle running down his cheek. 'Why not? She took Vee's place, didn't she?' he whined. 'As if she ever could, the ugly—'

Naomi drew her elbow forward, bent it at a hard angle, then rammed it back as hard as she could. She'd never deliberately inflicted violence on anyone before in her life, and as she felt her bone connect with the soft tissue of Rudy's gut, she felt a little sick, but there was no way she was going to let Riordan haggle with this man.

She just knew it would belittle him somehow.

She felt her head snap back as Rudy began to bend double, his breath expelling past her ear in a moist, horrible whistle, as he grunted in pain. Her vision swam dangerously in a tide of red and black and her neck seemed to wrench out of her shoulders.

But Rudy's grip was slackening, and she was able at last to drag in a much-needed, deep, unimpeded and wonderful gulp of air.

At the same time, Riordan shot forward, one hand reaching out for her, grabbing her arm and pulling her forward towards him and safety, whilst his other hand shot out towards Rudy, connecting with his shoulder and shoving him backwards.

Rudy tumbled over into the dirt, heaving. Curling up into a foetal position, he gasped and gagged.

'Are you all right?' Riordan cried, drawing Naomi to him, searching her blue eyes, her lovely, strong, brave face.

Naomi, not sure she could speak yet, nodded feverishly. She squeezed his arm and took several more gulps, desperate to reassure him. As long as he was with her, she was fine. And always would be.

Riordan looked past her to the man writhing in the dirt, then looked away, disgusted. He supposed he should feel sorry for Rudy. Obviously the man was mentally ill, just as his sister had been. But somehow, he couldn't conjure up any pity for him.

He brushed the damp blonde locks off Naomi's face, and watched her battle for composure.

Jago took a few steps forward, keeping one wary eye on the man on the ground. 'Don't tell me,' he said gruffly. 'Your brother-in-law.'

Riordan nodded.

Charis, now that the immediate crisis was over, shook her head in disbelief. 'He was at the party too,' she said at last. 'Do you remember, Jago? You ran him off when he started to get fresh with me. In the rose arbour.'

Jago stared down at the man, his face tight with contempt. 'Yes,' he said flatly. 'I remember him. Well, there's your thief,' he said disgustedly. 'He must have stolen the statue to try and set up Dr Vane.'

Charis nodded. 'And to think I blamed you,' she said softly.

She looked up at him, tears in her eyes. 'Did I ever apologize for that?'

Jago laughed. 'I doubt it.'

Charis grinned. 'Then don't hold your breath.'

Naomi slowly bent down, placing her hands on her knees, and took deep breaths. The black spots were all but gone now, but the heat and airlessness were taking their toll. She felt a little dizzy.

'Do want me to carry you?' Riordan said anxiously. 'Naomi?'

She straightened, shaking her head. He would never have to carry her, like he'd been forced to carry his first wife. She was utterly determined about that.

'No, I'm fine,' she croaked. 'Honestly, I feel much stronger already.'

Jago came over to them, glancing at Naomi, then at Riordan. 'Do you need help?' he offered. He was bigger than the volcanologist, although he doubted if he was much fitter.

'I'm fine,' Naomi croaked again.

And then, above them, the sky began to scream.

Or so it seemed.

For the sound seemed to just be there, with no warning, no rumbling, no nothing, just there, like a massive, solid, live thing.

And then the earth joined in – not in sound but in movement.

Charis fell first, stunned and disbelieving, the dry dust rising up around her as she hit the dirt. She instantly tried to get up, but couldn't, not even on to her knees.

It was like one of those fairground rides, where you stood on a platform which bucked and jolted under you, refusing to let you gain your equilibrium.

Beside her, Jago stumbled forward, cursing, whilst Riordan

grabbed Naomi, bringing her down on top of him, cushioning her fall. Even as he did so, he slanted his head upwards, seeing molten lava begin to overflow the crater, like a giant pot coming to the boil.

His first thought was about pyroclastic flow.

If that happened, they were all dead.

But even as he thought it, he knew it wasn't going to happen. He couldn't have said why, exactly, or offer any scientific data for it. He just knew.

But the lava flow was going to be fast. Very fast. For the highest elevation of the mountain was naturally steep, and the lava flow, like any moving, liquid force, would pick up momentum as it took the least line of resistance.

'Come on, get up!' he yelled, scrambling to his feet, all but yanking Naomi upright. 'We've got to run. Now!' he screamed.

Jago, now that the first stunning sound of the eruption was gone, and now that his eardrums had stopped thrumming, letting him get almost used to the massive noise, barely heard Riordan's words; nevertheless he reacted instantly, lurching upright, reaching for Charis, picking her up as if she was no more than a feather pillow, hoisting her high in his arms and looking around.

'Which way?' he screamed back at Riordan.

From his arms, Charis pointed immediately in the direction of the statue. 'Towards Pele!' she screamed, knowing that if they could only reach the *Heart of Fire* they'd be safe.

At the same instant, Riordan looked at the erupting crater, his agile mind calculating everything it was seeing and hearing, collating it with past eruptions he had studied, and coming up with the answer.

'This way!' he yelled, grabbing Naomi, who was white-faced but calm, and starting to run down the trail, which also lead to where the statue had been placed.

'Rudy, get up and run!' Riordan yelled at the man as they sped past him.

But Rudy didn't seem to hear. He was still lying on the ground, staring open-mouthed at the top of the crater.

Jago took off, Charis still in his arms. He supposed he must be afraid. After all, he was on an erupting volcano, smoke and ash and molten lava pouring down the mountainside, maybe even making right for him, if he only dared to turn around and look.

But he wasn't aware of fear. Or panic. Or really of anything much, except his pounding feet and the precious bundle in his arms.

Charis hung on tightly, staring over his shoulder, to where Naomi and Riordan, hand in hand, were running after them.

A little way back she saw Rudy Carter stumble to his feet and stagger up, but Jago was running so fast, his long legs eating up the yards, his feet unerringly finding the right path, avoiding the rocks, slithering sometimes down shifting rivers of pebbles, as sure-footed as a mountain goat, that Rudy was soon left behind and out of sight.

Once or twice Jago jerked and stumbled wildly, but she never thought that he might drop her, and he didn't. Her eyes went back, time and time again, to the top of the mountain, trying to see which way the lava was flowing. But it was impossible to tell.

At one point, she lifted her face to kiss Jago's neck, knowing words were impossible at this point, and wanting to touch him.

He was gasping heavily as the air became smoky, but not slowing at all, and she closed her eyes, holding on to him with all her might.

Well, if this was the end, at least they'd go together.

But even as that clichéd, bizarre, somehow strangely wonderful thought crossed her mind, she became all at once utterly calm.

Because she knew it wasn't going to happen.

They were rounding the corner that led to the road now, the various Jeeps looking flimsy but welcome in the distance, and she knew the statue was there, waiting for them.

And in her mind's eye, as her lover carried her to safety from the volcano and the molten death it was spewing, she felt as if someone else was with her.

A man, who'd lived long, long ago. A man who'd also been on a mountain, perhaps even this very one, when the lava had flowed and Pele had stirred. A man who'd lived to carve a statue from the heart of the fire goddess herself, a work of art so pleasing to her that Pele would never be able to bring herself to destroy it.

'The statue!' Charis gasped, as Jago, heading for the Jeep, sped past it. He cursed, backed up, saw Naomi and Riordan race past them, and ran to the statue.

Charis struggled out of his arms, grabbed the statue of the legendary fire goddess, and ran with him to the Jeep.

Once in the passenger seat, she looked back.

The mountain top had disappeared in a cloud of smoke and ash. Some of the ash was even now falling all around her, making her cough. Her eyes began to water from the pain, but even so, she couldn't see a river of fire, and knew that it wasn't flowing this way. Once again, the legend held true, and Charis gave up a brief but heart felt prayer of thanks to God for her safety, and then prayed for those others living beneath the mountain.

Naomi and Riordan's Jeep shot away.

And as Jago gunned his own engine, looking over his shoulder as the wheels spun and he reversed desperately, yanking on the wheel to point them downwards, then ramming the car into gear, his face running with dirty sweat, his steel-grey eyes fired with determination to live, and to live with Charis, Charis herself stared down at the statue in her hand.

She'd keep it safe always.

Chapter Thirteen

One week later, they all met up at the bar based at Riordan and Naomi's apartment building.

Charis looked wildly out of place in the rather downmarket room, dressed as she was in an exquisitely tailored, emerald green cocktail dress, with a wild profusion of night-scented jasmine weaved into her hair. But she and Jago were going on to a private party at a friend's house later, so she'd had no other choice.

Jago briskly ordered the drinks, beers for himself and Riordan, a cocktail for Charis, and fruit juice for Naomi, and took them to the small table, set well back in a dark, intimate corner. There he took a long swallow of his drink, watching Riordan do the same.

'You look beat,' Jago mused, glancing from Riordan to Naomi, and then back again. 'Both of you.'

Although still easily managing to look gorgeous in a pair of white shorts and a blue tank top, Naomi had dark smudges under her eyes, and her face looked pale. Beside her, Riordan looked, frankly, shattered.

Naomi smiled ruefully. 'You might say that. Kulahaleha has been leading us a merry dance. We think she might erupt again soon.'

'It's causing a problem,' Riordan agreed, 'because, naturally enough, the mayor and all the civic leaders are anxious to know when people can go back to their homes. With the tourist season in full swing, accommodation's at a premium, and nobody likes camping out in schools and gymnasiums for long.'

Jago nodded. 'And are you going to give them the all-clear?' he asked curiously.

Naomi and Riordan exchanged glances.

Charis watched the interplay, deeply impressed and touched by it. It was as if they were speaking to each other without words. But then, she now knew, they'd been together a long time, before they'd ever 'got together', so to speak.

Over the last week, Naomi and Charis had chatted every day on the phone, although Naomi's hectic work schedule had, perforce, kept the conversations short. Still, Charis felt as if the couple opposite were already her and Jago's best friends, and would remain so for the rest of their lives. It was as if the volcano had forged them all together, forming a bond which could never be broken.

It was one of the reasons Jago and Charis had invited themselves over. They had something very special to ask of the other couple.

'No, I don't think we are,' Riordan said, answering Jago's question at last. 'We're still getting some ominous rumbles and strange anomalies from the surface temperatures.'

'We're already having to rewrite some of the manuals,' Naomi said. 'The mountain really took everyone by surprise. Except Riordan,' she added, the pride in her voice apparent to all at the table.

Riordan actually blushed.

218

'Yes, well, it's certainly an interesting eruption,' he said, clearing his throat. 'All in all' – and here he glanced lovingly across the table at Naomi – 'I'm glad we came to Hawaii.'

Naomi smiled back at him.

Jago reached across under the table and squeezed Charis's hand.

'Well, we're certainly glad you came,' Charis said brightly, taking a sip of her drink. 'It was down to you that only one person was killed. The people who lived on the lava-flow side of the mountain only got out in time because they were ready for it.'

Jago nodded. 'I bet they were watching the mountain pretty closely after being notified of your warning.'

Riordan nodded, relaxing back into his chair. 'Yes. That, as you say, is the main thing. I hate it when a volcano takes a life.'

They were silent for a moment, contemplating Rudy Carter.

His body had been found by the emergency services two days after the erruption. He had not been burned, of course, because the lava flow hadn't reached him – but he had died from breathing the noxious gas.

They discussed him for a while, all of them wondering why he hadn't run. Riordan wondered if he'd refused to run in some kind of insane one-upmanship. It would be just like Rudy to think that he was being a better man than his brother-in-law by not fleeing.

Charis wondered if the poor man had had some sort of complete mental breakdown that had rendered him incapable of rational thought.

There was no doubt that he'd tried to ruin Riordan by stealing the statue. The man was already mentally ill, surely?

And now that the statue was back at Kokio Aloalo Palace,

where it belonged, neither she nor her grandfather were keen to publicize it's theft by telling the truth about a dead man. After all, Rudy was not there to defend himself. And, in a private conversation between the two of them, both had been inclined to think that the theft of the statue, and it's fortuitous placement at the foot of a volcano about to erupt, were facts best not examined too closely.

'So, I dare say you're going to be pretty busy from now on, then,' Jago said, ultra-casually, interrupting Charis's thoughts and winking at her outrageously as he took another swallow of his beer.

'Hell, yes,' Riordan said ruefully. 'We've got volcanologists coming in from all over the world, especially from Iceland. There are certain similarities between what's happening on Kulahaleha and an eruption there which occurred back in the seventies. Then there's the supervision of data collection system we've put into effect. It's a bit of an experiment, but it seems to be working so far. Then we've got to analyze the data, some of which we're still waiting on from the GPS system, and of course—'

Naomi, reaching across to take his hand, cut him off in midflow. He looked at her, one eyebrow raising in query.

'Not everyone's as fascinated about eruptions as us, sweetheart,' she said softly. It was the first time she'd used a term of endearment in public, but it slipped from her lips as freely as a bird took to the air, and Riordan liked it.

Then he assimilated her words, and briefly apologized to Charis and Jago, who smiled back their forgiveness.

'Besides, I rather think Charis and Jago want to talk about something else?' Naomi offered, having sensed the simmering excitement existing between the other two.

Charis took a deep breath. 'As a matter of fact, we do.' She looked across at Naomi and grinned. 'How do you feel about being a bridesmaid? And not just any old bridesmaid, but the chief?'

Naomi grinned all over her face, looking from her to the beaming Jago, then back again. 'You don't have to ask twice!' she assured her. 'When?'

'Next month,' Jago growled. 'If I had my way it would be tomorrow, but Charis insists she needs that long to prepare.'

'And so I do,' Charis said firmly. 'Grandfather wants to make a big splash. And, besides, being who we are, we probably wouldn't be able to get away with a simple private family affair anyway,' she said, merely stating a fact.

Jago groaned, but good-naturedly.

'You just wait until the press get wind of it,' Charis warned, 'as they're bound to. The dressmaker is sworn to secrecy, and thanks to you getting the rings from London, that's all taken care of, but once the florists and caterers are booked, it'll only be so long before it's splashed across the *Herald*. Then we'll have to invite the whole island along.'

Jago shrugged. So long as they got married, he didn't care if the whole world and its granny came to the wedding.

Jago glanced across at Riordan. 'My brother Keith's going to be best man, otherwise I'd ask you to do the honours,' he said, but Riordan was already shaking his head.

'Fine by me. I'm no good at speeches anyway!' He lifted his glass. 'To you. Long life and happiness.'

'Yes. I hope you're so happy together,' Naomi echoed, sure that they would be.

Her new-found friends were very different from other people she knew, and Charis was a little scary before you got to know her. Her vibrant beauty, and of course her title, created a false image of her as a good-time party girl. But

Naomi had come to sense a far more down-to-earth nature beneath the glamour, coupled with an almost spiritualistic sense of the world and approach to life.

And Jago, of course, was scary in his own right, and Naomi wasn't just thinking of his appearance now. Although, with his handsome face, highlighted by the scar, and thousand-pound suits, he created a formidable front, he also had all the hard-headed, sharp-witted skills of a self-made multi-million-aire to boggle your mind.

But Riordan liked him, and Naomi, although she'd personally run a mile from a man like him for herself, could sense that, together, Charis and Jago somehow made a pair.

Just as she and Riordan did.

As if reading her mind, Charis leaned forward and smiled secretively. 'So when are you and Riordan going to tie the knot?' she asked softly. 'Or is that none of my business?'

Riordan glanced at Naomi, silently giving his consent, and Naomi sighed happily. 'We thought the year after next,' she said, surprising Charis. 'I know, it sounds a long time,' Naomi said quickly, 'but really it's not. We'll have so much work to do here, and after next year our contract at the observatory will be up anyway. So workwise, it's an ideal time. Besides, we think it'll be good for us to wait. We've known each other so long as workmates, we want to have a good solid base as soul-mates behind us too, before we exchange vows.'

Jago caught the self-satisfied but unselfish look in Riordan's eye, and nodded in perfect understanding. After all, he knew just how the other man felt. When you finally met and won the woman of your dreams, what else was there to be except very, very happy?

'So, where are you going to get hitched?' he asked. 'In England?'

Riordan grinned and shook his head. 'No. We both agreed that Paricutin would be ideal,' he said.

Charis frowned. 'It sounds lovely, but I've never heard of it. Is it a desert island?'

Naomi laughed. 'No, it's a volcano,' she burbled. 'In February, in 1943, a small hole appeared in a cornfield in Mexico, near the village of Paricutin. Hot ash came from it and formed a small cone.'

'One day later,' Riordan took up the story with relish, 'lava flow came from the vent and continued to raise the level of the ground.'

'Two years later,' Naomi said, her face glowing as much as Riordan's, 'it was Volcano Paricutin, standing 1,640 feet above the level of the cornfield.'

'Just the perfect place to get married,' Riordan sighed. 'We'll find a local priest, and invite a few friends. So make a date in your diary for two years' time. Spring, perhaps?' Riordan said, looking questioningly at Naomi.

'Spring in Mexico sounds fine,' she agreed.

Jago looked at Charis and shook his head. 'They're hopeless,' he said, mock-sadly.

Charis and Naomi both burst into laughter.

Five weeks later, Jago ducked his head as Charis's cousin placed a *hei*, or crown, of plumeria flowers on his head.

He was standing in the grounds of Kokio Aloalo Palace, where swathes of flowers formed arches, and red carpets had been laid out, upon which rows and rows of chairs, filled with chattering guests, stood facing the towering cone of Kulahaleha, which was now calm.

At the back, press photographers clustered like hungry waifs and strays kept at bay by security men, whilst to the left, an orchestra began to play 'The Wedding March'.

Jago stiffened, and turned. In the front row he saw his mother, sniffling into a handkerchief, her eyes bright with happiness and tears, dressed in powder blue and looking every inch the proud mother of the groom. Beside him, as best man, Keith gave his mother a cheerful grin.

But Jago's eyes quickly moved on, over the sea of guests, Riordan and Naomi's faces included, towards the house, and the open French doors, where, beside her grandfather's wheelchair, Charis had just appeared.

Everyone turned to look as she walked forward towards them, and there was a collective gasp.

She was dressed in brilliant white, with a garland of bright flowers in her hands, and another hei on her head. Through the white lace veil, her raven hair and the flowers glowed with colour and life.

She glided towards him, petite, proud, incredibly beautiful, and Jago took a huge breath as she drew level with him.

She looked at him through the veil, her dark brown eyes twinkling mischievously. He'd confessed to her, only yesterday, that he was nervous. He, who was never, ever nervous!

She hadn't believed him then.

Now, as her grandfather reached up to take her small hand and place it on to his, she squeezed his hand tightly.

Jago nodded.

And, together, they turned to face the preacher.